In the dream, Wil had a chance to save Tara...

Even though she'd committed suicide, by some cosmic miracle, she was alive and standing in front of him with a gun to her head, which was bizarre in itself since she'd died by hanging.

A phone rang and he knew if he answered it, Tara would pull the trigger. But what if it was the station and they had an emergency? Even in the dream, he realized the thought was crazy. His wife holding a gun to her head was an obvious emergency.

Still, he let his gaze flick to the phone. When he turned back to Tara, she was gone and Abby stood in her place.

Now he leaned more toward ignoring the phone and felt guilty about choosing Abby over Tara.

"Please don't," he said in a strangled voice and even though he knew he was dreaming, he was also aware he'd spoken out loud, because he could feel the strain in his throat.

The ring became more shrill and his eyes snapped open. He looked at the alarm clock. Two-fourteen a.m.

He fumbled for the receiver and lifted it to his ear. "'allo," he mumbled into the mouthpiece.

"Wil? It's Lesli."

"Lesli? From the station?"

"Yes. I need you to come down to the beach. Komano Bay."

He rubbed a hand over his face, trying to clear away the last vestiges of the dream. "What is it?"

"I'd rather not say until you get here."

"What the hell happened?" he demanded, now wide awake.

There was a pause, then, "It's your daughter."

Tears of the Wounded

by

Alicia Dean

Tears of the Wounded

Cover Art by *Kim Mendoza*

The Wild Rose Press
PO Box 708
Adams Basin, NY 14410-0706
Visit us at www.thewildrosepress.com

Publishing History
First Crimson Rose Edition, 2008
Print ISBN 1-60154-286-0

Published in the United States of America

Dedication

For Mike

Chapter One

His hands, slick with perspiration, trembled as he reached for the ammonium nitrate. Sweat beaded his forehead and trickled into his eyes.

He stopped and took a deep, calming breath, trying to get his nerves under control.

Why should *he* be nervous? Teddy was the one who should be nervous.

Theodore William Garrett.

He knew a lot about Theodore. He'd studied him long enough. Theodore's father had given him the name because he was a baseball fanatic and Ted Williams was his favorite player of all time. Theodore's parents were both dead now, his mother from cancer and his father, a year later, from a heart attack.

Theodore married his high school sweetheart, Tara, and they had a child, Lindsey. Lindsey was now a motherless fourteen-year old. Theodore currently had a beautiful girlfriend, even prettier than his lovely, deceased wife.

Theodore always seemed to come out on top. But that was about to change.

He'd waited a long time to make Theodore pay.

Well, it wasn't like he'd been totally idle. He'd

kind of screwed with him already. Like, that shit with his wife. Talk about fucking up somebody's day.

But, he'd more or less been picking on Theodore. Kind of like a bully on a playground who takes a smaller kid's lunch money. In truth, Theodore was the bully. Theodore had stolen much more than his lunch money.

He could have taken Theodore out years ago. But what do they say? Revenge is a dish best served cold?

Death would have been too quick, too easy. Almost merciful.

No, he had something much worse in mind for Mr. Theodore William Garrett. The woman and the child were the keys. They were pawns. Instruments. Spoils of war.

He would make Theodore sorry he'd ever been born and he wouldn't rest until he'd avenged her death.

Yes, that's it. *The Avenger.* He was The Avenger.

He bent over the tiny plastic case. The work was very tedious, very precise. But the object had to be small.

Another cliché came to mind.

Dynamite comes in small packages.

He laughed, his sweat drying in the cool air of the dimly lit room.

He was no longer nervous.

Chapter Two

Abby Bishop lifted her face to the sky, reveling in the taste of salt water on her lips, the cool sea air blowing through her hair, and the warm sun caressing her skin.

"Male dolphins are called *bulls* and female dolphins are called *cows*," Abby told the six passengers of her Blue Harbor, Florida dolphin-watching excursion.

Abby's gaze drifted to the girl who sat in the seat next to her in the cockpit. Lindsey Garrett was pretty, with wide, hazel eyes and perfect skin, only slightly marred by adolescent acne. The teenager's long, dark hair was pulled back in a ponytail, but beyond that, Lindsey made no attempt to look fourteen. She wore a nose ring and flip flops, a tight pink spaghetti strap shirt, and booty shorts that showed her butt cheeks.

If she'd been Lindsey's mother, Abby never would have let her out of the house dressed like that. Abby knew Wil didn't like it, but he sometimes let it slide, and Abby was in no position to tell him how to dress his daughter.

Abby had been dating Wil for over a year but

3

had only recently met Lindsey. The girl didn't seem to like her much, so Abby was pleasantly surprised this morning when Wil called to say Lindsey wanted to come along on one of her tourist trips.

So far, the girl hadn't said a word and her expression hadn't changed from one of abject boredom.

Maybe it was because they hadn't spotted any dolphins yet. They didn't always, but Abby had about a ninety percent success rate and prayed this would be one of those times. She didn't want to acknowledge it, but she was trying to impress Wil's daughter. Trying to win Lindsey over.

"Dolphins can't live long out of water because their bodies overheat. They communicate via a series of—" Abby stopped, her breath stalling as she spotted them, about a hundred yards off the port side.

She did this for a living and had seen dolphins hundreds of times, but the sight never failed to leave her momentarily speechless. In a breathy voice, Abby said, "There." And pointed toward the beautiful creatures. Two of them broke the surface at that precise moment, perfectly in sync.

Oohs and aahs arose from the passengers, a couple with a ten-year-old son, and three young men who looked to be in their early twenties. But Lindsey didn't move, didn't respond. Her gaze flicked to the dolphins, then back to Abby.

"The sounds are a series of whistles and clicks called phonations," Abby went on, keeping the twenty-six foot Bayliner even with the dolphins without getting any closer. One of the most important aspects of her excursions was not disturbing or harming the creatures. "Dolphins use their flippers to make sharp turns and sudden stops."

Lindsey spoke up. "What about the mating

rituals of the dolphin?"

Momentarily disconcerted, Abby cleared her throat, then said, "Well, their courtship sometimes involves bumping heads. Most of them mate in spring and early summer and—"

"My dad, like, has so many girlfriends it's insane," Lindsey interrupted. "I just wondered if dolphins were man whores, too."

Abby nearly gasped. Not so much at her words, but at the malevolence in the girl's eyes. Abby's face heated and she purposely avoided meeting the gazes of her other passengers.

"If you'll watch, the dolphins will periodically leap from the water, normally in twos, while those behind them swim just under the surface, then take their turns cresting the water," Abby continued, not responding to Lindsey. She wasn't sure what to say next. It was a good thing she had her spiel down pat, and an even better thing that Lindsey didn't speak again.

Abby didn't really think Wil had other girlfriends. He didn't seem the type to cheat and the two of them spent a great deal of time together. Even if he did date other women, it wouldn't be a big deal. She cared about him, but they weren't necessarily in a committed relationship.

What bothered Abby about Lindsey's comments was that the girl felt the need to make them, in front of others who might or might not guess Lindsey was talking about the man Abby was dating.

The intentional attempt to inflict pain, to cause conflict, was what troubled Abby. She'd seen enough conflict in her life, encountered all the trouble, all the violence and mayhem she cared to. She also didn't want to cause Lindsey problems. God knew, teenage girls had enough already. Especially Lindsey, having found her mother dead from a suicide four years earlier.

And, selfishly, Abby didn't want to deal with an angry, resentful daughter fighting for her father's attention.

The remainder of the cruise was mostly silent with Lindsey casting smug glances at Abby.

When it was over, Abby guided the boat into its slip and helped the passengers disembark. As Lindsey passed by, she smiled at Abby and swiped her hands together, as if brushing off dirt.

To Abby, the gesture seemed to say, 'My work here is done'.

****

"Got a live one, wanna take it?" Sheriff Ray Roberts asked, stopping next to Wil's desk, his hands resting on his protruding stomach.

"You know I don't go out on calls anymore," Wil said.

"Not even for a gigantic set of silicone hooters?"

"Come again?"

"Marlo Swain called. Seems she was sunbathing and a couple of boys stole her top. I told her to stay like she was so we could recreate the scene."

Wil laughed and lifted his hands, miming a typing motion. "No longer my job description."

After his wife died, Wil had given up his job on the bomb squad of the Miami PD so his ten-year-old daughter wouldn't have to worry about losing another parent. He'd moved here to Blue Harbor and taken a job as a deputy where the worst crimes were—well—stolen bikini tops. When Lindsey's bad dreams and sleeplessness persisted, Wil switched to a desk job. With her father completely removed from the line of fire, Lindsey had slowly improved.

"Nothing but a desk jockey now?" Ray asked.

"I'm leaving the tough cases to the rest of you."

Ray snorted. "Don't remind me. How we gonna handle those big ole fake boobies?"

Marlo Swain was a widow who lived in Blue

Harbor during the fall and winter months. Her wealthy husband had passed away a few years ago, leaving her well off and large-breasted.

"You seem pretty sure they're not real. You have firsthand knowledge?" Wil said, grinning as Ray's face reddened.

"They're about as real as Barry Bonds' home run record." The sheriff sighed and looked around the room. "Guess I'll have to send Lesli, since she's the only female. Ronald would be so embarrassed he'd have a coronary and Prescott would tamper with the evidence."

"I'm sure whoever you send is up to the challenge."

"Yeah, I know, I know. The only boobies you're interested in are Abby's. Bet those are real, huh?"

"Hey, watch it."

"Aw, come on. All I can do is talk about 'em. Give me something."

Wil shook his head. "You're nothing but a dirty old man. Your ass should have been in a sling a long time ago."

"Guess it's cause I look like goddamned Wilford Brimley," Ray grumbled.

This was true. With sparse hair and a mustache as white as a fish belly, round, gold-rimmed glasses, and cheeks that were perpetually rosy, he could pass for Wilford Brimley...or Santa Claus.

Wil's cell phone rang and he looked at the caller ID. Abby. Wil flipped open the phone and mouthed to Ray he needed to take the call and Ray wandered away.

"Can I see you today?" Abby asked.

"With or without clothing?"

She laughed, but it sounded forced. "With."

"Is something wrong?"

She was silent, then, "I just need to talk to you."

"Is everything okay with Lindsey?"

7

"Lindsey's fine. It's not about her."

"Want to come by the station? I'll be here another hour or so."

"No."

Wil felt like an idiot. He'd momentarily forgotten Abby was as vehemently opposed to police work as Lindsey. Abby had been reluctant to even go out with him until he'd convinced her that the biggest danger he faced was carpal tunnel syndrome and paper cuts. He figured there was a story behind her fear, but she never talked about her past and he didn't push.

"Can't you tell me on the phone?" Wil asked.

Silence again. He heard her take a deep, shaky breath, like she was trying not to cry. "I didn't want to do it this way."

Wil had that panicky flutter in his chest he'd had the day Lindsey called him, crying hysterically, from her grandpa's cabin. He'd had it again the first few times Lindsey's screams woke him from a deep sleep.

"Abby? What's going on?"

"I can't see you anymore. I'm sorry. It's just not working out for me."

The panicky feeling traveled from his chest to his hairline. "Tell me what happened." His throat felt raw and tight.

"Nothing happened," she said wearily.

"You owe me an explanation." Now he was pissed. *Great, that's sure to change her mind.*

"There's no explanation to give you. I was reluctant to get involved with you in the first place, with anyone, for that matter. It's just been too much, too fast. I can't do this. I'm sorry. Goodbye, Wil."

"Abby?"

She was gone. Wil snapped his phone closed and looked around the room. Ray was talking to Lesli, no doubt sending her out on the call. Latham Prescott hovered nearby, gesturing with his hands. Wil figured he was trying to talk Ray into letting *him* go. Ronald was pouring a cup of coffee, probably relieved that whatever was going on didn't involve him.

No one was looking in his direction. Pressing his fingers against his closed eyes, Wil was relieved to find them dry...relieved he was only crying on the inside.

****

The bar was one of those out of the way places...dark, shabby, without the calypso music and island trappings of the other, more touristy establishments. Even its name was unpretentious, 'Jerry's'.

The Avenger scooped a handful of nuts from the bowl on the bar, fed them into his mouth via the opening between his thumb and index finger, then washed them down with a Samuel Adams.

Pulp Fiction played on the TV hanging behind the bar. "Can you switch that to the news?" the Avenger asked the bartender.

The guy was fat with a goatee and long gray hair tied back with a leather cord. He held up a chubby finger. "Hold on, pal."

Pal. He hated that. It had never bothered him until he heard a comedian on television say, to him, pal was the same as fuckface. He hadn't thought of it that way before. Now that he did, he couldn't stand it.

"Sorry," the bartender said, still holding up a finger. "Gotta see this part."

The movie was at the scene where Samuel L. Jackson quoted a bible scripture just before he blew some guys away. The bartender said it with him, word for word, ending with, "And you will know my name is the Lord when I lay my vengeance upon thee." He chuckled and shook his head. "Man, that Samuel L. Jackson is one badass son of a bitch."

9

No, motherfucker, I'm a badass son of a bitch. Samuel L. Jackson is just playacting.

The bartender picked up the remote. "Here's your news, pal. Not a lot going on."

There sure wasn't. Not like there had been when he and Wil lived in Miami.

He watched the blonde anchorwoman drone on about the happenings, her expression never changing from wide-eyed delight whether she was talking about Jet Ski races or the war in Iraq. She was cute but sucked at reporting the news. Maybe she sucked at something else, and that was how she'd gotten the job.

A photo of Mayor Bingham flashed on the screen. Mayor Micah Bingham—former Miami Chief of Police, Wil's best friend, and the man who had condoned Wil's actions—was speaking in a public forum one week from today.

Vulnerable. Exposed.

He took another swig of the Sam Adams and gave a satisfied burp, wiping his mouth with the back of his hand.

The news just got interesting.

Chapter Three

The sun sank into the Atlantic, leaving behind a purplish pink trail in the sky. Wil tilted his chair back, propping himself up with one foot on the deck railing.

The ocean was still tonight, its surface like a sheet of sapphire glass. Slow moving lights in the distance cut a path through the dusk. A boat. It made him think of Abby. Not that he didn't already think of her 24/7. He'd done the same when they were together.

Then, thoughts of Abby had given him a thrill that was part affection, part lust. Now, since she'd broken things off two days ago, thoughts of Abby depressed the hell out of him.

The worst part was not knowing *why* she'd ended things. He knew she valued her independence, her freedom. She was leery of commitment. But he was more than willing to take it slow, give her all the space she needed. He thought he had. Now this.

He took a sip of mango tea. The sweet, fruity taste coated his mouth and seemed to stop at the knot of pain resting at the base of his throat. Feeling a little nauseous, he set the tumbler on the table

11

next to him.

The glass doors slid open behind him and Lindsey stepped out onto the deck.

"Hey, punkin'," he said over his shoulder.

"Hey, Dad. Whatcha doing?"

'Daddy' had disappeared about the same time as her baby fat and he missed it. She wore a tight shirt that revealed cleavage she was just starting to develop. Her pajama pants were rolled down until they rested just above her pelvis. Come to think of it, he missed the baby fat, too.

"Just hanging out," Wil said. "Wanna join me?"

She flopped down in the chair next to him. Mimicking his pose, she rested her feet on the deck railing. Her flip flops were made of tiny pink seashells and her sparkly toenail polish glittered in the moonlight.

Without looking at him, she said, "You miss her, don't you?"

She'd asked that question a lot over the past four years, and it had always referred to her mother. She hadn't asked it in a while, and he figured now she was talking about Abby. Either way, the answer was the same.

"Yes." He looked out over the deck to the water, lest his expression give away just how *much* he missed Abby.

Lindsey didn't speak and he turned his attention back to her. She stared down at her hands in her lap and twisted a silver ring with a large black stone around her finger.

"It's my fault," she said, in almost a whisper.

"What's your fault?"

"Abby breaking up with you."

Wil's brows drew together and he dropped his feet from the railing. "Where did you get that idea?"

"When we were out on the boat. I said some things." She took a deep breath. "I was kind of an effitch." Effitch was Lindsey and her friends' term for effing bitch. He was pretty sure that, when no adults were around, Lindsey and her friends just went with fucking bitch. "I kinda said you had other girlfriends."

Wil thought about it for a moment. Abby wouldn't have believed that, or at least he didn't think she would. She knew him. They had a good thing together. She wouldn't let a snide comment by a fourteen-year-old break them up. If nothing else, she would have asked him about it. There had to be more.

"What else did you do?"

She shrugged. "I think maybe she just didn't want to deal with me. I was, like, pretty rude."

Wil felt a rush of anger at his daughter he'd never felt before. Not just the usual exasperation. Actual anger. "Why would you do that?"

Lindsey's voice rose defensively. "I don't like her. She's, like, *around* all the time. And she's all phony nice."

Wil ground his teeth, trying to keep his temper under control. "She's not *phony* nice. She's genuinely nice."

Lindsey snorted. "Yeah, right. You think that cause you're doing her."

Wil frowned and said sharply, "You watch your mouth, young lady. That was uncalled for."

"Sorry," Lindsey muttered under her breath.

"Why did you decide to tell me this now?" Wil asked.

Lindsey did some more ring twisting, not looking at him. When she spoke, the hint of tears in her voice made her sound like the little girl she'd been not long ago. It helped to ease Wil's anger. "The last time me and Mom were at Grandpa's cabin, it rained. I asked Mom what rain was made of." She gave a small laugh that ended on a swift intake of breath. "I was bored 'cause I couldn't go outside. I just wanted Mom's attention. Wanted to talk about something. Mom said, 'Rain is made from tears of the dead.' I said, 'But, Mommy, the dead don't cry.' She was quiet for a long time, then she said, 'You're right, honey. The dead don't cry. Rain is from tears of the wounded.' I asked her how they got wounded and she gave me this really sad look."

Lindsey drew in a ragged sigh as tears filled her eyes. "Mom said, 'We're all wounded, Lindsey.' I'll never forget that look on her face. Her eyes were far away, kind of dead." Tears streamed down Lindsey's face as she launched herself into his arms, taking him by surprise. She buried her face in his neck, her words muffled. "You had that same look when I walked out here, Daddy. I don't want you to be wounded. I'm so sorry. Please don't be wounded."

Wil held her and stroked her hair, feeling tears well in his own eyes. "Shhh, sweetie. It's okay. I'm fine. Daddy's fine. Don't worry."

He knew the time she was talking about. He remembered because that was the weekend Tara had killed herself and left their ten-year-old daughter to find her body. After it happened, he'd hated himself for not being there. He'd been working that weekend, which was the norm. He'd also hated Tara for leaving them alone and putting Lindsey through that. And somewhere, way down deep inside his grief-ravaged soul, so deep he'd never acknowledged it, just a little, he'd briefly, unreasonably, hated Lindsey for not preventing it.

Lindsey pulled away and looked at him intently through eyes that were red-rimmed and wet, although the sobs had stopped. "Did I ever tell you I dreamed I heard a man's voice that night? It seemed so real I actually convinced myself he was there. In my head, I made up this whole story about how *he* killed her. How Mom didn't commit suicide because she would never leave us like that. I think I did it to keep from feeling guilty for letting Mom die."

Wil's heart clenched. He should have been there. Should have protected his wife and little girl. He reached out and took one of Lindsey's hands, squeezing gently. "It wasn't your fault, sweetie. Don't think that for a minute. Your mother was a very sad woman. I just didn't know how sad, or I never would have let you go away with her. It's not your fault."

She nodded and wiped at her cheeks, her many rings clinking together with the motion. "If you want to hook back up with Abby, I'll stop being rude to her. I still won't like her, but I'll be cool. I swear."

Wil smiled. "You do know that, no matter what, I'll always love you, always be here for you. No one can change my love for you and no one can take your mom's place. Abby wouldn't even try."

"I know." She leaned down and kissed him on the cheek. "Night, Dad."

****

Abby bent over in her leather office chair to tie the strings on her sneakers. She had a tour in an hour and, for the first time since she'd started the business, her heart wasn't in it. She missed Wil already.

It was funny, but one of the things she missed most was his hugs. He had these firm, warm hugs where he'd wrap her in his strong arms, pull her to his chest and she'd feel like nothing bad in this world could touch her.

She'd never had much security, growing up, or in adulthood. Her life had been filled with changes, with moving from place to place, making new friends, starting new careers, never really feeling like she belonged.

But when Wil held her, it felt as though she'd found a haven. It felt as if she'd come home.

"You can't go out today."

Abby straightened and looked at Diane, her friend and receptionist. Diane's blonde hair, piled on top of her head in a black scrunchy and teased until it resembled a bird's nest, bobbed as she typed rapidly on her keyboard. The clicking of the keys was barely audible above the alternative rock music coming from Diane's radio.

"Why not?"

Diane stopped typing and leaned back in the chair, folding her arms. "You're so miserable, the sharks will smell it and circle the boat, go on a mad feeding frenzy."

"It's blood that attracts sharks, not misery," Abby informed her dryly.

"Yeah? Well you're bleeding misery all over the place. The sharks might get confused." Diane's face brightened. "I have an idea, why don't we go out? Get drunk and get you laid? You know what they say, the only way to get over a man, is to get under another one."

Abby rolled her eyes. "I'm not in the market for another man." Abby hadn't been 'in the market' when she'd met Wil. But the attraction had been like a tidal wave and she'd dove in head first.

"Well, you should be. Don't get me wrong, I like Wil, but I don't like to see you unhappy and I don't want you to be alone."

"I'm going to miss Wil, sure. But I don't need a man to make me happy. I'm fine."

"Still, it would be fun to go out. How about Friday? Perry and Wil are supposed to play basketball." She grimaced. "If the two of them keep hanging out, it could get...awkward."

"Don't let it. I don't want what happened with me and Wil to cause problems with you and Perry, or with their friendship."

Behind her, Abby heard the door open. She

turned and her mouth went dry, her heart thumping in her chest.

Wil stood just inside the room. He wore an open-necked black shirt and khaki pants. The light coming through the window caught the strands of gray in his dark, curly hair. He smiled, flashing even white teeth. Laugh lines crinkled at the corners of his hazel eyes. The sight of him stole her breath.

"Abby," he said, quietly, tentatively.

She didn't respond as he stood there, silently waiting.

"Hey, Wil. How's it going?" Diane said, finally breaking the tension.

He flicked a glance at Diane but his gaze was on Abby when he spoke. "Okay. You?"

"Fine. I, uhm, I need to—there's something outside I..." Diane trailed into a mumble and stepped around Wil to leave the office, giving them some privacy.

"Lindsey told me what happened," Wil said once they were alone. "I'm sorry and so is she. From now on, she'll show you respect. She's going to apologize, too."

Abby shrugged. "It's not necessary."

"Yes, it is. I don't know exactly what she did, but if it upset you that much, she owes you an apology."

"It didn't."

"But you ended things because of it, right?"

Abby shook her head. "No, that's not why. Well, not entirely. What happened with Lindsey just made me realize I shouldn't be in a serious relationship. Especially not with someone who has a child."

His brow creased. "What does that have to do with anything?"

Abby had never really talked about her past to Wil. She shared some of it now, but only a small part. "My mother remarried when I was about Lindsey's age. I hated my stepfather and my teen years were hell at best. I was in all kinds of trouble. I wouldn't wish that on Lindsey." She smiled. "You know, the crazy thing is, my stepfather was a good guy. I just didn't like that mom replaced my father so soon after he died, so I never gave him a chance."

She didn't tell him that her mother had been seeing Ross *before* her father died. She supposed, as always, she was dealing with Wil on a 'need to know' basis. It didn't say a lot for their relationship, nor her ability to be in a healthy one.

"You're talking about your mother and *stepdad*. You didn't think I was going to marry you, did you?" He gave her that lopsided grin that never failed to buckle her knees, and her heart constricted.

Determinedly ignoring his attempt to lighten the conversation, she said, "Lindsey lost her mother and she's probably afraid she'll lose you, too. Her attitude is understandable."

"I told her she wouldn't. She's fine with the idea of us being together now."

"I'm sorry, Wil, I need my life to be simple. I don't deal well with complications. Even though Lindsey says she's fine, you didn't see the hostility." She met his gaze. "Did she say she wants me in your life?"

He opened his mouth, hesitated, then sighed and didn't answer.

"That's what I thought," Abby said quietly. "No matter what she says now, there would be problems down the road. I'd just rather not deal with that. And I'd rather not screw up her teenage years, or cause you the tension and stress that comes along with it. I need peace."

Wil narrowed his gaze and asked softly, "What makes you so afraid of life?"

In her mind, Abby saw the blood, heard the gunshot, felt the agony once more. But she only shook her head. She couldn't tell Wil. Couldn't talk about it to anyone. She'd buried that part of her past and wanted it to stay buried. "I'm sorry, Wil. It's over. I need to go. I have a tour in a few minutes."

Wil's mouth tightened and a muscle worked in his jaw, but he nodded his acceptance. "Okay. I won't bother you again."

Chapter Four

The walls of the club were covered in grass to give the illusion of a tropical hut and palm tree centerpieces sat on the tables. 'Kokomo' by the Beach boys played on the jukebox. One thing Wil had soon learned after moving to Blue Harbor was everywhere there was music, you could expect a heavy dose of Jimmy Buffet songs, 'Don't Worry, Be Happy', and the soundtrack from the movie *Cocktail*. Kenny Chesney, with his plethora of island songs, was quickly earning his place among Blue Harbor's musical repertoire, as well.

"Assholes want to pass another goddamned smoking ban." Ralph, the owner, leaned his hands on the bar, his knuckles white with tension. "Fucking government wants to tell me I can't let people smoke in my own goddamned bar. And the sonsabitches say I have to wear a goddamned seat belt. Who are they to tell me how to live *or* how to die?"

Wil grinned at Perry. They'd heard this same tirade every time they came into 'Blue Bombay' and still chose it as their after-game hangout.

Tonight, they'd had to forfeit due to lack of

players. City employees made up their team and two of the firemen had been called to an emergency. Perry worked maintenance for the city.

"Maybe it's because seatbelts are good for you and smoking is bad for you," Perry suggested.

"Yeah?" Ralph's voice rose. "Cheeseburgers and candy bars are bad for you, but you don't see those fat motherfuckers trying to ban those."

Wil looked at Perry and shrugged. "Guy's got a point."

Ralph slapped his meaty hands on top of the bar. "*That's* what I'm talking about." He slid another drink over to Wil. "This one's on me."

Wil thanked him, then breathed in a lungful of endangered smoke hovering in the air and lifted the Crown and Coke to his lips. He glanced up at the TV behind the bar.

ESPN was showing spring training highlights and predictions for the upcoming baseball season. Wil had wanted to be a major league ballplayer at one time, but, after getting beaned by a ninety mile an hour fastball in college, he'd decided baseball was a spectator sport. He didn't have the talent, anyway, so it was just as well.

Perry slid off his barstool and walked over to the window, peering outside. Wil knew he was checking to make sure his 'baby' was safe. Perry had a 1970 red Firebird he'd restored to mint condition. He obsessed about it, made sure it was locked up like state secrets, and set the high-tech alarm if he planned to be away from it for more than ten minutes.

"Hey, look who's here," Perry said.

Wil looked up to see Abby and Diane walk in the front door. His chest tightened as he looked at Abby. She was gorgeous in snug black pants and a shimmery silver-white blouse that showed a little more of her bronze flesh than he would have liked.

Alicia Dean

Her hair, the color of rich caramel, hung loose and silky around her shoulders.

Lust tugged at his groin and jealousy sat like a hot stone in his throat. Every man in the place had to want her.

Wil slid closer to the bar in an attempt to conceal his erection. Not easy to do in cotton athletic shorts.

"Didn't know they were gonna be here, did you?" Perry asked.

Wil shook his head. He wouldn't have come if he had. Seeing her and not having her was just too damned hard.

The women took a table toward the front of the club, not looking in Wil and Perry's direction. Wil swiveled back around to his drink to keep from staring at Abby.

"I'll go over and say hi in a minute," Perry said. "Hey, do you know that guy?"

Wil broke away from his morose contemplation of the ice cubes in his glass. "What guy?"

Perry nodded toward the back of the bar. "The dickhead over there in the corner. The one with those gay flowers on his shirt."

Matt Bingham, the mayor's brother. Even though Wil and the mayor were good friends, his brother hated Wil's guts.

Matt had been in love with Tara. He blamed Wil for her death, and for being married to her when Matt wanted to be. Wil didn't think anything had ever happened between Matt and his wife, but he couldn't say for sure. Wil had worked long hours during his marriage and Matt's feelings were pretty intense not to have been reciprocated.

"He's giving one of us the eye," Perry said, pushing out his chest. "I think he wants to go. Better not be me he's looking at, I'll break him in half." Perry jerked his head toward Matt and a lock of his hair fell over his forehead in a curly-Q that looked like the tip of a soft serve cone.

Wil laughed at the thought of Perry breaking anyone in half. Perry was more funny-looking than intimidating. He was tall and lanky, with arms about as big around as drinking straws.

"Calm down, Bruiser," Wil said. "I think he's glaring at me."

Just then, Matt shot Wil a smug look and Wil met his stare briefly. Matt smiled as he rose from his seat and worked his way over to the table where Abby and Diane sat. Wil didn't think Abby knew him, but he wouldn't put it past Bingham to use being the mayor's brother as his pick-up line.

Bingham leaned down, resting a hand on the bare skin of Abby's back. Wil tensed, wanting to punch the guy's face in. Abby discreetly shook off his touch and Wil released the breath that had jammed in his throat.

"He's scheming on your chick," Perry said.

Wil shrugged. "She's not my chick." He stood and tossed a ten on the bar. "Gotta run."

"We should stop and say hi to the girls."

Wil glanced back at their table. Matt was no longer talking to them. He'd retreated to his cubbyhole, but his eyes still followed Wil.

"Sure."

As they approached the table, Abby looked up and met his gaze. Her eyes, the same shade as her hair, usually held a glint like sunlight through honey. Tonight they were shadowed by sadness, or maybe that was just wishful thinking.

Her stare seemed to shoot straight to his soul. His gut clenched and a tingle moved up his spine. Hoping his voice didn't betray his emotion, he said, "Sorry, I didn't know you'd be here. The game was cancelled."

She smiled. "It's okay. We're bound to run in to

each other from time to time. I don't want it to be weird between us."

Wil returned her smile, or at least tried to. His body was wound so tight, he wasn't sure his lips cooperated. "Neither do I." He nodded at Diane. "You ladies be careful. I gotta run."

He left Perry talking to the women, walked out into the cool night air, then took in a deep breath and released it.

He wished it were that easy to release Abby from his mind.

Chapter Five

Somewhere nearby, a radio played.

No, not a radio, a television. A sitcom, but one Abby couldn't identify. She tried to open her eyes, but couldn't. Her tongue felt too big for her mouth. She swallowed, but all she managed was a dry clicking sound that hurt her throat.

Finally, she forced her eyes open and found herself staring at a water-stained ceiling. When she turned her head to the left, she saw a window covered by thick drapes with a sliver of light showing between the panels. She scowled. Where was she?

"You're awake."

She gasped. The voice came from her right. It was coarse, deep and staticy, as if filtered through a speaker. She turned her head toward the voice and knew immediately she was in trouble. If she weren't in trouble, the man sitting next to the bed probably wouldn't be wearing a hooded sweatshirt and a *Friday the 13th* Jason Voorhees hockey mask.

Tears rushed to her eyes and she tried to speak, or maybe scream, but the inside of her mouth was coated with something dry and sour and she couldn't.

"Here." He stood and bent over her, placing a wet cloth to her lips. "I'd let you drink water but you might vomit and I don't want to clean it up."

She hesitated. What if he was trying to poison her? But if he wanted to kill her, he wouldn't have to trick her. She was pretty much at his mercy already.

She parted her lips and greedily sucked moisture from the white terry cloth. He pulled it away after a few seconds.

"Who are you?" she asked, her voice sounding almost as raspy as his.

He spoke again, and it was then she realized he had one of those voice-altering boxes. It made him sound like Darth Vader.

"Rule number one, you don't ask the questions, I tell you what I want you to know and I call the shots. Rule number two...see rule number one." He laughed, the sound distorted and eerie. "I've always wanted to use that line." He picked something up from the nightstand. "Now that you're awake, first things first." A pair of handcuffs dangled from his fingers. He snapped one end to her right wrist and the other to the metal rail of the headboard.

"What are you...?" She struggled, jerking at the restraint. A sharp, burning pain ripped through her lower abdomen. She gasped, reflexively putting her free hand on her stomach. In terror, she looked at her captor. "What have you done? What's going on?" Her voice rose in hysteria. "What do you want?" She tried to calm herself, but sobs tore at her throat, intensifying the now searing pain in her stomach.

"You need to chill out. You're not helping matters by getting hysterical. I told you, no questions, but I guess you're entitled to a few answers. But first, you have to calm down. I'll give you pain medication shortly, after we've talked."

She took a deep breath, willing away the tears,

willing away the terror.

Apparently satisfied, he continued, "You've had minor surgery—"

"Surgery?" Confusion filtered in with the fear. Had there been an accident? She looked around the room again. Definitely not a hospital room. And she was wearing the same clothes she'd worn to go out...was it last night? "I don't understand. You're a doctor?"

"No, but I did stay at a Holiday Inn Express last night." Again, the eerie laughter. "Sorry, couldn't resist. But seriously, no, I'm not a doctor. I didn't do the surgery myself. I enlisted the help of a man who was once a doctor. A man who had his license stripped a few years back but still practices for a few bucks under the table. Kind of a shady character, but a competent physician."

The confusion clouding her mind increased. She took a deep breath, trying to clear her thinking, to calm herself. It didn't help. She could smell her own sweat and the sour odor of fear. She recognized the fear. She'd felt it six years ago when she'd watched her husband murdered in front of her eyes.

Think, Abby, think.

The last thing she remembered was being at the bar with Diane. They'd had a few drinks, maybe too many, because most of the night was fuzzy. She didn't remember leaving the bar...had no idea what had happened

"Diane...?"

"Your friend from the bar? She's fine. I watched you two. Waited until she got you home. Then, I broke into your house and took you. Easy peasy."

"What do you want?"

"You'll find out soon enough." He cuffed her other hand to the rail. "I will tell you, I don't have a beef with you. It's your boyfriend. You're just a pawn in my quest to bring Wil to justice. A tool, collateral

27

damage, whatever you want to call it."

"Wil? Why?"

He heaved a deep sigh. "You don't listen, do you? I said, no questions. You'll know what I want you to know when I want you to know it."

She fell silent, her horrified mind trying to grasp what was happening...and why.

He leaned over her and she saw the syringe in his hand.

"No, please." She shrank back, but there was nowhere to go.

"I've got to leave for a little while and I need to know you won't be discovered."

She felt a sting, then a burn as the liquid entered her veins. He stuffed a handkerchief in her mouth.

"This is to keep you quiet, not that there's much danger if you do yell. I just like to err on the side of caution. No one to come to your rescue, even if you could scream for help. You're in one of those out of the way places where screaming is not uncommon."

He said more, but she didn't catch it. His words faded away, as did the room.

****

The Avenger sat on a bench at the outdoor skating rink, his eyes on the kids rolling along under the stars to the beat of a song by a female pop singer. He thought it might be Avril Lavigne, but wasn't sure.

He wore black framed glasses with lenses so thick they distorted his eyes, making him look like Don Knotts on acid. He'd shoved a Florida Marlins cap over his brown hair. A fake mustache completed the look.

Lying next to him on the bench was a pair of shoes—blue flats such as a young girl might wear—and a pink canvas bag with 'Kelsy' spelled out in black glitter. Inside the bag was a pair of binoculars,

28

a knife, and a Beretta. He couldn't decide which weapon to bring, so he'd brought both.

A plump but pretty thirtyish mother, also holding her child's belongings, sat beside him. They'd already discussed what a handful pre-teen girls could be, but agreed they wouldn't trade them for the world, God love 'em.

"Which one is Kelsy?" she asked him now. Her daughter was Amy and she had proudly pointed her out a few minutes ago.

He craned his neck as if searching for his daughter. "You know, I don't see her," he said, forcing concern into his voice. At that moment, Lindsey and her friend headed toward the back of the rink where the food and beverage vendors were set up. He grabbed the shoes and bag and stood. "I better go look for her. You can't be too careful, you know. The things that happen to young girls these days." He shook his head and tut-tutted. "Nice meeting you," he threw over his shoulder as he walked away, then made a show of searching the sea of teenagers for his fake daughter, while keeping Lindsey and her friend in his sights. Man, if being a real father was even half this much work, he wanted no part of it.

He saw the girls slip past an Italian Ice vendor into an area that spilled out onto the beach. They were moving rapidly now and he picked up his pace and followed.

By the time he reached the spot where they'd exited the skating area, they were midway down the beach. It was darker out here, the half moon barely giving off enough light to make out the figures hurrying across the sand. He stayed in the shadows, close enough to keep an eye on them, but not close enough to give away his presence.

The girls stopped beneath a pier near the water and he ducked behind a pile of brush thirty feet away.

What were they doing out here? He didn't think it was parentally approved, whatever it was.

He took the binoculars from the bag and brought them to his eyes, focusing just in time to see the flame of a lighter touch the tip of a cigarette.

Lindsey, you naughty girl.

So, they'd come out here to smoke. Which meant they probably wouldn't be here long. He'd have to make a move soon. This would likely be his best opportunity. And he needed to get it over with. He didn't like leaving Abby alone at the motel. It made him nervous that she might be discovered. Of course, with sedatives, handcuffs, and a gag, even the most unruly of women could be tamed.

What to do about the friend? He didn't want to hurt the other girl. She wasn't part of this, wasn't tainted with Theodore's blood. But, he might have to. He didn't see another way.

About the time Lindsey finished the cigarette, he heard the low roar of a small motor, getting louder by the second. He swung the binoculars around and spotted a three-wheeler approaching along the sand. Two guys were on it. Young, maybe early twenties, white teeth gleaming in their smooth, tanned faces.

They stopped next to the girls. *Uh oh.* Could be trouble. If these guys started hassling Lindsey and her friend, he might have to pull a rescue mission, *then* hit the girls.

But no, as he watched, the boy on the back climbed off and went over to Lindsey, giving her a hug. Lindsey's friend slid on the motorbike behind the driver and the two of them took off, waving to the couple left behind.

Another dilemma. Lindsey still wasn't alone. However, unlike his hesitation about hurting Lindsey's girlfriend, he wouldn't mind taking this asshole out. The guy had to be at least twenty, and he was messing with a fourteen-year-old. That wouldn't do. Just wouldn't do at all.

Slipping the knife out of the bag, The Avenger moved quietly along the darkened beach, coming up behind loverboy.

The guy had a hand up Lindsey's shirt and was feasting on her neck, but she didn't seem to be enjoying it. Her eyes were open and the look on her face was that of someone passing a kidney stone.

When Lindsey saw The Avenger, her eyes widened in fear and her mouth made a little 'o' of surprise. Loverboy hadn't heard his approach. He was too busy making like a vacuum cleaner on Lindsey's young flesh.

The Avenger lifted his index finger to his lips in a shushing gesture and winked like he and Lindsey shared a secret. Then, he brought the knife up and plunged it into the back of loverboy's neck. The guy groaned and dropped to the ground like the recipient of a George Foreman uppercut.

Lindsey released the scream she'd been working on and The Avenger quickly clamped a hand over her mouth. He slapped the chloroformed rag over her face, covering her nose and lips. She slumped, and he slung her over his shoulder, then quickly carried her back up the beach.

Chapter Six

In the dream, Wil had a chance to save Tara. Even though she'd committed suicide, by some cosmic miracle, she was alive and standing in front of him with a gun to her head, which was bizarre in itself since she'd died by hanging.

A phone rang and he knew if he answered it, Tara would pull the trigger. But what if it was the station and they had an emergency? Even in the dream, he realized the thought was crazy. His wife holding a gun to her head was an obvious emergency.

Still, he let his gaze flick to the phone. When he turned back to Tara, she was gone and Abby stood in her place.

Now he leaned more toward ignoring the phone and felt guilty about choosing Abby over Tara.

"Please don't," he said in a strangled voice and even though he knew he was dreaming, he was also aware he'd spoken out loud, because he could feel the strain in his throat.

The ring became more shrill and his eyes snapped open. He looked at the alarm clock. Two-fourteen a.m.

He fumbled for the receiver and lifted it to his ear. "'allo," he mumbled into the mouthpiece.

"Wil? It's Lesli."

"Lesli? From the station?"

"Yes. I need you to come down to the beach. Komano Bay."

He rubbed a hand over his face, trying to clear away the last vestiges of the dream. "What is it?"

"I'd rather not say until you get here."

"What the hell happened?" he demanded, now wide awake.

There was a pause, then, "It's your daughter."

Panic beat at his mind and his heart raced. He jumped out of bed, yanking a pair of jeans on over his boxer briefs, the phone trapped between his ear and shoulder. "Was she in an accident?"

She couldn't have been in an accident. She was spending the night with Alyssa. There was no way anything could happen to her at two o'clock in the morning.

"No, not an accident." She paused again. "She's missing."

He struggled into a T-shirt, headed out the door and slid into his pickup, the phone still at his ear as he backed out of the drive and pulled onto the road.

"Missing? From Alyssa's house? How?"

"No, not from Alyssa's house." A sigh. "Come to Komano Bay. You'll see the cruisers. I'll explain everything when you get here."

"Lesli..." He could hear the tremble, the desperation, the terror in his voice.

"Wil, are you going to be okay to drive?"

"Yeah," he told her, but he wasn't so sure. The lights along the causeway were like yellow-white laser beams shooting at him, then blending into the night, into the other cars whizzing by.

Wil felt a rush go through his body, like a balloon releasing air inside his rib cage. His heart thumped painfully, and hysteria was quickly winning over his fight to stay calm.

His daughter was missing. Something had happened to his baby girl.

Once again, he hadn't been there to stop it.

****

In just under ten minutes, Wil arrived at the beach.

He left the keys in the truck and barely took the time to close the door as he rushed through the cool night air toward the flashing lights spraying reds and blues out over the water.

Lesli had her back to him, but he recognized her standing with a couple of the male deputies a few feet beyond the cruisers.

Wil ran across sand that felt like molasses, hearing Lesli's loose jacket flapping loudly in the wind, the only sound he could detect as he zeroed in on his target. When he reached her, he grabbed her by the shoulder, turning her to face him.

"What happened?"

Before she responded, he looked past her to where an ambulance sat, not moving. Yellow crime scene tape cordoned off an area about ten by ten around the pier. A figure was lying still in the sand.

"Oh, God." He shoved past the officers toward the body. They'd told him she was missing, not...

"Wil, wait." Lesli followed, grabbing a handful of Wil's T-shirt, momentarily halting his progress. "It's not Lindsey. It's a young man who was with Lindsey."

Wil looked again and saw that the figure was indeed male. He wore white athletic shoes and blue jeans with a dark-colored shirt. A wet pool glistened in the white sand beneath his head. Blood.

"With her?" Dazed, he looked back at Lesli. "She was with Alyssa. Not this guy. You've made a mistake."

Lesli's gaze dropped to the ground, then moved further up the beach where a small group of people stood. Wil recognized Alyssa.

Leaving Lesli and her protests, he rushed over to Alyssa. Lindsey's friend sobbed and trembled, rivers of black mascara streaking her face. A man around the same age as the dead guy stood a few feet away. His face was white and pinched and he had his arms folded over himself. His lower lip was lined with half a dozen small gold hoops. A bar pierced the area between his lower lip and chin, and it vibrated with his quaking. Tears and snot dripped over the metal.

Wil grabbed Alyssa by the upper arms. "Where's Lindsey? What happened?" When she didn't answer, he gave her a shake. "Alyssa, tell me where she is!"

Alyssa shook her head. "I don't know," she sobbed. "Oh God, he's dead."

"Yes. I'm sorry. Your friend is dead." He took a deep breath. "But, Alyssa, where is Lindsey? Where the hell is my daughter?" In spite of trying to stay calm, the last words ended on a roar and his grip tightened on Alyssa's thin arms.

"I don't know," she screamed, seeming to focus on him for the first time. "God, I don't know." Her sobbing increased in volume and Wil felt her tremble beneath his fingertips. "My mom and dad are going to kill me when they get here. Oh, God, I'm so dead."

Wil felt someone approach from behind, but didn't turn around until Lesli tugged on his arm. He let her pull him away, his wild gaze searching through the throng of people gathering on the beach, praying that, by some miracle, one of them would be Lindsey.

****

"A-bb—y, oh, A-bb—y...wake u-p!"

The singsong voice penetrated her drug induced sleep.

35

Eyes still closed, she frowned, an elusive memory just beyond her consciousness. It was as if a thick curtain had dropped over her mind and she almost knew what was on the other side, but not quite.

Needles of pain like tiny bee stings worked through her hands and arms. Her wrist bones ached and the flesh around them felt tender, raw.

Suddenly, the curtain lifted. She knew exactly what was on the other side.

Reluctantly, she opened her eyes. A hockey mask hovered a few inches above her face.

"Good, you're awake. Can't sleep the day away. We have a lot to do." He straightened and dropped into the chair next to the bed, resting his elbows on his knees. "Now, here's what's going on. The surgery was to install a tiny device in your lower stomach."

"Device?" she croaked.

"Yes. An explosive device."

She sucked in a breath, a gasp that was more like a sob. "What? What are you talking about?"

"I know. Sucks, doesn't it? But as long as your boyfriend does as I say, it should be okay. You're an insurance policy, although, actually, I have two."

"Two?"

"You'll find out about the other soon enough. For now, we need to take care of the business at hand. If you'll stop interrupting me, we can get this over with more quickly. Just so you know, it won't do you any good to try to have surgery to remove it. I've also placed a transmitter beneath your skin that measures body temperature. Anesthesia lowers your body temperature. If there is a change, a remote device I have beeps. So, unless you want that thing cut out with no anesthesia, I'd advise you to leave it in."

Her body trembled, terror making black spots appear in her vision. Shallow breaths emitted from her chest, like a dog panting from heat stroke. "Oh God," she moaned. "Oh God, oh God."

"Enough! Calm down and listen to me. If everyone plays by my rules, you have a chance to survive. If not, you're fucked. Your life, and those around you, depends on your lover. He holds your fate in his hands." He held up a bag. "You need a shower first off. I mean, you already smelled like a bar when I brought you here. You've been lying here for thirty-six hours and that catheter isn't the most sanitary way to relieve yourself. I removed it and emptied your bag, but, bottom line, you smell. I brought you some clothes." He dropped the bag on her stomach. "I'm going to be in the bathroom while you shower."

"No!" she shouted, although she wasn't sure why the thought was so abhorrent to her after everything else she'd suffered.

He shook his head. "Trust me, I'm not going to go all sex crazed on you. I just want to make sure you don't figure out some devious trick to get away before I'm ready for you to."

He stood and, reaching over her head, unlocked the cuffs. The tingles became more intense and tears welled in her eyes as she rubbed her wrists.

"Okay, you can get up and we'll go to the bathroom. Be careful about your incision while you shower. Need to keep it as dry as possible."

For a moment, she just lay there, trembling. She wondered what her chances were of making it to the door if she rolled off the opposite side of the bed. He stood between her and the bathroom, but the door was—

"Don't even think about it," he said, as if he'd read her mind. Maybe she'd cut her eyes toward the exit, even though she hadn't meant to. "You're weak, the door's locked." He gave an amused snort. "You have a goddamned explosive device in your intestines, for which I have a detonator. Where the hell do you think you're gonna go?"

Nowhere, she thought desperately, hysteria crowding her throat. This was a fucking nightmare, an unbelievable, fucking nightmare.

When she still didn't move, he reached down and grabbed her arms, pulling her from the bed. He released her as soon as her feet touched the floor and she stumbled, her legs almost too weak to support her. The room tilted crazily and she thought she might fall, but was afraid that if she did, he'd touch her again.

"It'll take a little while for your strength to return," he told her almost kindly. "But you'll be fine."

He led her into the bathroom and twisted the knobs on the shower. "I'll turn around while you get in, but only for a second, so you'd better hurry."

When his back was to her, she quickly stripped and stepped into the bathtub, jerking the plastic curtain closed. The hot spray felt good on her battered body, but terrified tears coursed down her cheeks, mingling with the water as she scrubbed with the motel soap. She used the shampoo and washed her hair, moving on autopilot.

When she finished rinsing, she spoke through the curtain. "Can you please leave while I dress?"

"I won't watch," he said, giving an impatient sigh. "Just hurry."

She peeked around the curtain and saw that his back was still to her. She jerked a towel off the rack and dried quickly. From in the tub, she took the clothes he'd hung next to the towel rack and pulled them over her still damp body.

He'd brought her pink sweat pants that said 'juicy' on the butt and a white T-shirt that was a few sizes too small. She had no bra; the blouse she'd worn last night hadn't required one. She crossed her arms over her chest and stepped out of the tub onto the tile. "This shirt is too tight," she told him.

He turned back to her. His eyes gleamed with something that sent a wave of revulsion over her skin and a rush of fear from her hairline to her toes. Even through the holes of the mask, she could see the glitter in his eyes. *Dear God, he'd said he wouldn't...*

"Looks good on you," he said, not touching her or making a move toward her. "It'll have to do."

She didn't argue further, knew it wouldn't do any good. She dried her feet and slipped on the socks and white tennis shoes he'd brought. Surprisingly, the shoes were only a little too big. Other than the shirt, he'd done an amazing job at guessing her sizes.

"Come on," he commanded and she followed him to the motel door. He told her to turn around, and when she did, he tied a blindfold over her eyes. "I'm taking off my mask," he said. "Don't want to freak out the people who might be around."

She heard him open the door, and as they stepped outside, he spoke in a voice that sounded almost familiar, but she couldn't place it. She had a feeling she should be able to recognize it. She must know him, otherwise, why the disguise?

"Sorry, honey," he said loudly for the benefit of anyone nearby. "It's a surprise for your birthday. You can't see where we're going til we get there."

He helped her into the car and they drove for perhaps twenty minutes before stopping. The car door opened, and she felt his hand on her arm as he pulled her out. He walked her a few feet, then pushed down on her shoulders. She sat on a hard surface and he pressed something into her hand. A cell phone.

"Wait ten minutes after I drive away and call Wil. If you remove your blindfold or use the phone before I'm completely out of sight, I'll detonate the explosive."

She heard his footsteps retreat, heard the car door close and the engine accelerate as he drove away.

She began to count off the minutes in her mind. *One thousand one, one thousand two, one thousand three...*

She wanted Wil now, needed him desperately, craved the warmth of his embrace. But she would wait. Even though doing so was almost as agonizing as everything else she'd been through, she would wait. Her kidnapper had told her to wait ten minutes.

Just to be sure, she waited twenty.

Chapter Seven

Wil had only been asleep for a few hours when he'd gotten the call about Lindsey early Sunday morning. It was now just past noon that same day. He'd had two hours sleep in the past twenty-nine. His eyes were gritty and raw, as if he'd been staring into a sand storm. His heart seemed to be made of lead and his mind felt like it would never rest again.

The house was quiet. Lindsey had been the main source of noise and now that she wasn't here, the only sound was the occasional gurgle of the coffee pot.

Wil went to the carafe and poured his fifth cup of coffee. He took a swig and felt it burn to the center of his gut. He hadn't eaten, so the coffee rumbled through his empty belly, making him queasy, but he needed the caffeine.

He'd gone to each and every one of Lindsey's friends. He'd talked to Alyssa's parents and learned that they'd been out and their eighteen-year-old daughter was supposed to pick up the girls. The parents had gotten home just after midnight, thinking the girls were tucked away in Alyssa's room. They hadn't bothered to make sure.

41

Wil had talked to the people at the skating rink and to the vendors around Blue Harbor Plaza. He'd come up empty. Not a hint, not a clue, not a whisper.

He'd even intruded on the grief of Birch Caulfield's parents. They didn't know Lindsey. They hadn't even known their son was dating a fourteen-year-old girl. Wil wanted to hate the kid, but his murder had taken that away.

Wil's cell phone rang and he yanked it from its case and flipped it open. "Hello?"

"Wil?"

The voice was watery, weak. It sounded like a little girl. He almost said, 'Lindsey?', but Lindsey wouldn't call him Wil.

"Oh, God, Wil," she sobbed and he knew who it was.

"Abby? What's wrong?"

"Can you come get me, please? I'm at the back of Atlantic Bank."

"Isn't the bank closed?" he said inanely. "I mean—"

"Yes," Abby gritted, now sounding impatient as well as distraught. "I'll explain everything when you get here. Please, can you just come get me?"

"Yeah, sure. Are you okay?"

She didn't answer his question, instead, with a tremble in her voice, she said, "And Wil? Please hurry."

****

Wil pulled into the back of the bank's parking lot and Abby was there, sitting on a bench the employees used for smoking. She rose quickly to her feet when she saw him.

She wore pink sweatpants and a tight white T-shirt. Her hair blew loose across her face, the sun picking up the gold highlights in it. Her arms were folded across her breasts. When he reached her, she dropped them and he saw why she had them crossed. She wasn't wearing a bra and her nipples were clearly defined beneath the thin T-shirt. Under normal circumstances, he'd have found the sight a huge turn on. But his daughter was missing. And something had happened to Abby. Although he didn't know *what* had happened, he could see the effects of her ordeal. Abby's face was bare of makeup and its glow had dimmed. Her skin looked sallow and dark smudges surrounded her eyes.

They stared at one another for a few seconds, then her eyes brimmed and tears spilled down her wan cheeks. Her lower lip trembled. He reached out and her body, soft and warm, fell into his. He closed his arms around her. She smelled of soap and some floral shampoo. He rested his chin on top of her silky head and inhaled deeply. It felt so damn good just to hold her.

"What happened, baby?" he murmured.

She pulled away and wiped her eyes. "Get me out of here. I'll tell you on the way."

He helped her into the passenger seat and went around to the driver's side.

He needed to tell her about Lindsey, but first, he'd hear her story.

****

Wil pulled out onto the road and Abby let her eyes drift shut for a moment. The motions of his pickup were oddly soothing, the large machine gliding effortlessly along the street. Abby clung to the normality of the situation, the dozens of times she'd ridden alongside Wil coming back to her, helping to ease her anxiety.

He reached across the seat and took hold of her hands where they rested in her lap. She knew he was waiting for her to speak, but she couldn't seem to find the words. Finally, she blurted, "I was kidnapped."

She felt Wil's hands tense on hers. "You what?"

His voice shook, maybe from shock, maybe from rage. Most likely from both.

"I was kidnapped," she repeated, more forcefully now. "I woke up in a motel room...a man..." She stopped, shuddered, took a breath and said, "A man had me in a motel room."

"Jesus." Wil whipped the truck over to the side of the road and parked on the shoulder, leaving the engine idling. He turned in the seat, raking a hand through his hair. "What did he...did he...rape you?"

Abby shook her head. "No. He didn't hurt me."

Not really, not unless you consider the fact that he cut me open and put a bomb inside me.

She didn't know why, but she couldn't quite say the words. Not yet.

While she'd waited for Wil at the bank, she'd lifted the edge of the bandage and looked at her incision. It was no more than an inch long. Amazing how something so small could cause such pain. Such terror.

"Then why? What did he want?"

She turned to look at him. "You."

His brow furrowed. "Me? What are you talking about?"

She told him everything then, except the information about the explosive. That was so bizarre, so frightening, so repulsive, she wanted to put it off as long as possible. During the telling, she kept her head down, her gaze fixed on the hands clasped in her lap.

"Good God," Wil exploded when she finished.

Abby lifted her head to look at him. Wil stared out the windshield, his face drained of color, his eyes wide with shock, looking like the victim of a horrific accident.

"Can you take me by my house to change?" Abby asked when Wil didn't make a move to leave.

He nodded and put the truck in drive, pulling

out onto the road. "He knew me, then?" he said quietly. "He did this because of me?"

"That's what he said. He wants you to do something, I guess. He said if you'd cooperate, everything would be okay."

"You didn't recognize anything about him? You don't have any idea who he is?"

Abby shook her head. "No. He was well disguised. He used some kind of voice altering box. Even when he spoke with his normal voice, I couldn't recognize it. It sounded familiar, but I think maybe he still tried to disguise it."

Wil nodded, not speaking, seemingly in deep concentration.

When they arrived at Abby's house, her guts clenched. She was reluctant to go inside and that only increased her anger at the bastard who'd done this. He'd invaded her home, had made it a place of fear rather than a shelter.

Wil followed her through the door and Abby looked around, not seeing any sign of struggle or forced entry. Her house was neat and tidy, the plaid sofa cushions in place, the knick-knacks on the gleaming surfaces of the cherry wood coffee and end tables looking undisturbed.

Surely she hadn't been that drunk, that he could take her so easily. Had she been drugged?

In her bedroom, the aqua blue and chocolate brown comforter was wadded, her sheets wrinkled. He'd actually snatched her from her *bed*. How could she possibly have been unaware of something like that?

She tried to put her mind to that night, tried to remember...but she couldn't. She had absolutely no recollection of anything that had happened. Didn't even remember leaving the bar.

Pulling her gaze from the bed, not wanting to think of what he might have done to her, she changed into jeans and a white sleeveless blouse. When she entered the living room, Wil was seated on the sofa. He stood and looked at her solemnly, his eyes filled with guilt and concern.

"There's something I need to tell you," he said.

She nodded but when he didn't speak right away, a flutter of panic went through her heart. "What's the matter?"

Wil shoved his hands in his pockets and stared at her with a look of ragged agony.

"Wil, what is it? What's wrong?"

"Lindsey's missing," he said, his voice raw with emotion.

"Missing?"

"Someone took her. Late last night—early this morning, actually. Murdered the boy she was with. It almost has to be connected with what happened to you."

An icy wind chilled her insides. "It *is* connected. This is what he meant."

Wil's eyes narrowed and he took her gently by the shoulders, staring down into her face. "What he meant by what?"

"He talked about a backup insurance policy. He must have meant Lindsey."

"Jesus," Wil whispered, then released her and shook his head. "What does the bastard want? Why let you go?"

Abby sighed and crossed her arms around her middle. "He has an insurance policy for that, too."

"What do you mean?"

"He implanted a device. An explosive device. Inside me."

Wil's eyes widened and his face tightened with disbelief. "Good God...what..." He shook his head and lifted his hands helplessly. "How..." he broke off and once again shook his head, his hands now hanging limply at his sides, as if all the air had left his body.

"It's a small explosive. In my abdomen. He has a detonator and if you don't do what he wants..."

"No. That can't be." Wil suddenly seemed infused with energy. "He's just trying to scare us. We need to take you to the hospital, have you checked out. And if it's true, we can have it removed. Right?"

She shook her head. "Wrong. He made sure of that. He also had a transmitter placed underneath my skin. It measures body temperature. If I go under anesthesia, he'll know. He'll detonate the explosive."

****

Reeling from what Abby had told him, Wil reached out and gently lifted her shirt just far enough to look at her stomach. His gut clenched when he saw the white gauze against her tan flesh. He ran a trembling finger over the edges, touching the rough bandage, then her soft skin. As if seeing it made it more real, he felt a lump rise in his throat. He blinked rapidly, fighting the tears, and dropped her shirt back in place.

Wil had never felt more helpless in his life. His daughter was missing and Abby had been... God, he couldn't even get his mind around what the son of a bitch had done to her. And, the most frightening thought of all...the psycho who'd done this horrible thing had his little girl. What might he do to Lindsey?

A tingle started between his shoulder blades and moved up through the back of his neck. His chest constricted and he had to struggle to draw oxygen into his lungs. He was losing it. He didn't know what to do next, where to turn.

"Wil?" Abby's concerned voice broke through his thoughts. "Are you okay? You look pale."

"Yeah." He clenched his teeth and took a deep breath. "I'm fine. Listen, we need to make sure everything he told you is true. The fewer people who know about this, the better, but we need to take you to the hospital for an x-ray. Maybe if I tell them it's official police business, they'll be discreet."

"I know who can help. My stepfather is a surgeon at St. John's."

"Here? Your parents live here? You never told me."

She shrugged. "I guess it never came up."

They'd been together for a year. That was the sort of thing that should 'come up', but it was just another part of Abby's life she'd closed off to him.

"We also need to go by the police station. You should give them your statement."

Her eyes widened and she put a hand to her lips. "I don't want to..." she shook her head. "It's so awful, so humiliating."

"Hey," Wil reached out and squeezed her hand. "You didn't do anything wrong. You were a victim. This son of a bitch has got to be stopped. We need to inform the authorities."

She nodded and Wil slid a hand underneath her hair, cupping the back of her head, then placed a kiss on her forehead.

"Now, let's go take a look at your insides."

Chapter Eight

On the drive to the hospital, Wil continually scanned the streets and sidewalks for any sign of Lindsey. Each time he saw a girl his daughter's age, his heart would speed up. But it wouldn't be her. It never was.

He and Abby had gone by the sheriff's department first and Abby had given her statement to Ray, closed up in his office with just the three of them there. The older man had been gentle and understanding with her and Wil was grateful to him for that.

The receptionist at the hospital, a thin woman with large brown eyes and an upper lip badly in need of waxing, looked up when Wil and Abby stopped at her desk.

Abby gave her name and asked for Doctor Novak. The receptionist picked up the phone and made a call, then replaced the receiver and said, "Go to the sixth floor. The doctor will be waiting for you."

Wil and Abby rode the elevator in silence, Abby with her back to him, staring up as the lighted numbers counted away the floors. No one joined them on the way. St. John's Hospital wasn't exactly a bevy of activity.

The elevator doors slid open seconds later and, as promised, Abby's stepfather was waiting for them when they stepped off. He wasn't at all what Wil expected. Wil had pictured someone tall, distinguished, someone who looked like a surgeon.

Ross Novak was barely 5'6. Fat bulged from his neck down, as if a giant hand from above had squashed him and everything pushed outward. Wispy brown hair sprouted from his nearly bald head. His homely face lit up when he saw Abby.

"Abby, my dear! How wonderful to see you." He held out his pudgy arms and Abby hesitated, then stepped forward for a brief hug.

"Ross, this is Wil Garrett," Abby said. "Wil, my stepfather, Ross Novak."

Wil grasped the man's hand in a quick handshake.

"I'm afraid this isn't a social call," Abby told him. "I need a favor."

"Anything, my dear. Anything at all."

Abby explained everything, including what had happened to Lindsey, and Wil saw the color drain from the man's face, his jovial expression melting like a sno-cone on a hot griddle.

When Abby finished, Ross wiped tears from his eyes and hugged her again, this time longer, but gentler. "What do you need me to do?" he asked when he released her.

"The first thing we'd like is an x-ray. We want to make sure this creep is telling the truth and not just bluffing."

Novak nodded. "Come with me."

He punched the 'down' button on the elevator and the three of them stepped in. They rode to the second floor where they followed Novak down a hallway and through double doors that read 'Laboratory and X-rays'. Novak introduced them to

Don, a middle-aged, Native American man in a white lab coat.

Novak explained what they wanted and Don took Abby through a door while Ross and Wil waited in an adjacent room. Neither of the men sat. Wil paced while Novak stood with his hands in the pockets of his lab coat, staring at the floor.

"I'm sorry about your daughter," Novak said softly.

Wil stopped pacing, a new and sudden pain gripping his chest as the realization washed over him once more. It was strange that sometimes he could almost forget Lindsey was missing. Then, when awareness returned, a bout of guilt and grief ten times stronger than the previous one would suffuse him.

"Thanks," he managed to say through the tightness in his throat.

Novak raised his head and looked at Wil. "I never had children of my own, although I wanted them. When I married Charlene, Abby's mother, Abby was eleven. I thought she was the most amazing, most beautiful child on earth and I felt somewhat like a new father must feel when his baby is brought into the world. I couldn't imagine loving a child of my own any more than I did Abby." His smile was pensive. "Abby didn't take to me right away. Still hasn't, really. But I adored her. I know she resented me because Charlene and I married just a few months after her father died. Can't blame the kid. I tried to be the best father I could be. We moved here to be close to Abby, just in case she needs us. You know, after what she went through. I don't see her much. Not nearly often enough. She and her mother go to lunch once a month or so and I see her when she comes to pick Charlene up. On holidays, we sometimes get together. I'd hoped for more, but what can you do? Giving her that boat didn't even make a difference."

Wil didn't know what she'd been through, or what boat Ross referred to—he was pretty certain Abby herself had purchased the Bayliner—and he didn't ask. Now wasn't the time to ruminate Abby's past with her stepfather.

Ross's gaze moved to the wall that separated them from the room where Abby was being x-rayed. "I can't imagine what she must have been feeling," he said quietly. "The terror she experienced. I'd die if anything happened to her." He looked back at Wil. "You have to help her. Please."

"I will."

"You love her?"

Wil hesitated. He'd never actually said the 'L' word to Abby. Not really. Six months into their relationship, he'd told her he thought he was falling in love with her and she'd said, 'Please don't.' But he had, he'd just never brought it up again. She couldn't stop him from admitting it to her stepfather. "Yes. Very much."

Ross gave a quick, satisfied nod. "You let me know how she does. If she needs anything, call me. She won't call me, but you will, okay?"

Wil promised that he would. The door opened and Don came in, holding a large manila file, his expression grim.

Wil didn't have to wait for Ross to look at the films to know what he'd find.

****

Lindsey was in her own bedroom. Well, not the bedroom in Blue Harbor, but the one she'd had when she was younger. The one at her grandpa's cabin, where her mom had died. It looked different now that it was empty, but she knew it was her bedroom. The pink carpet and lavender walls were the same.

The cot she sat on was the only piece of furniture in the room and she could see the section of carpet she'd burned when she was eight and had lit her trash can on fire by throwing matches she'd just blown out into it. She wasn't trying to burn anything, she just liked the smell of matches.

Mom had been really pissed, but only for a little while. Lindsey could tell she was mostly scared. They had pushed her dresser over the charred circle and Lindsey had almost forgotten about the incident until she saw the evidence now.

She stood and paced around the room, rubbing her hands up and down her arms. It wasn't really cold, but she felt cold anyway. What was she doing here? How could this asshole get into her grandpa's cabin? Dad had sold it after Mom died. Had this freak bought it?

She crossed her arms over her boobs. The shirt was way too low-cut. Her Dad would spaz if he saw her in this. She'd worn it for Birch.

Thinking of him made a pain shoot through her stomach and to her chest.

Oh God, Birch.

He was dead. The asshole had stabbed him. She began to tremble and went back to the cot, lowering herself on shaky legs. Great sobs tore through her, and she clamped a hand over her mouth, not wanting to bring the man into her room.

She closed her eyes and tried to think of Birch alive, not like she'd seen him last. He'd been lying on the beach. She'd seen the blood just before she passed out.

Opening her eyes again, she pushed the sight from her mind. She wouldn't dwell on that, she'd think happy thoughts. Thoughts about the first time she'd seen Birch when he'd been hanging out with Alyssa's older sister, Amber.

Lindsey had immediately developed a big-time thing for Birch, right then, like love at first sight or something. She never thought he'd notice her, a fourteen-year old girl. But he had, and she'd been sooo excited.

Then, he'd wanted her to meet him at the plaza. Every chance they got, which wasn't often since her Dad kept such close tabs on her, Lindsey and Birch had snuck away to hang out. It was, like, the second time she'd hung out with him that he kissed her. She thought she'd died and gone to heaven. Each time, they'd gone a little further. Far enough, really, to kind of scare her.

She hadn't liked what he was doing to her last night. That had felt creepy, but at least she had an older, hot guy who wanted to be with her. She figured she'd get used to the other. But now she'd never know, because he was dead.

She closed her eyes and tried to stop crying. She couldn't think about that now or she'd go nuts. She had to figure a way out of here. She'd already tried the door and it was locked. Her window that had an awesome view of the ocean was boarded up.

She went to the door and tried it again, even though she was sure it was still locked. Her cell phone was gone. He'd probably taken it. She was screwed. Totally screwed. The tears she'd pushed back came now. Like a never-ending fountain, they streamed down her cheeks, spilling onto her neck and chest.

She was so freakin' scared.

Calm down, Lindsey. Your dad will find you, you know he will.

Yes, she knew he would. But would he find her before she was raped...or killed?

She heard a clicking, jiggling noise, then the door opened and *he* came in. He was tall and goofy looking. The thick glasses made him look like a nerd. She'd find his appearance amusing, if she didn't know what he was capable of.

She backed away, staring at him until she felt

the cot behind her knees. She dropped onto it and once more crossed her arms over her chest. She'd felt kind of sexy dressed this way when she'd been with Birch. Now, she felt like a slut and this asshole seeing her in this shirt gave her the creeps.

He smiled like he knew what she was thinking.

"How you doing, Lindsey?"

He knew her name. That meant he'd kidnapped her on purpose, not just grabbed some random girl. Why?

She didn't answer him.

"You hungry?"

Again, she stayed silent.

He shrugged. "You don't have to talk, you don't have to eat. You just have to stay here and be a good girl so that I don't have to kill you."

He said it nonchalantly, like he was telling her it was a sunny day outside.

"My Dad will kill *you*," she told him, with more fear in her voice than threat.

He smiled. "I'm not scared of Daddy. He'll be groveling on his knees before this is over with. It's his fault, anyway, so you should be pissed at him, not me."

He stepped toward her and she scooted further onto the bed, wrapping her arms around her chest again.

"Don't worry, I'm not going to touch you. But the way you're dressed, I hope you know you're asking for it. You look like a little whore and if your dad really cared about you, he'd make you act and dress decently instead of like a two-dollar hooker."

"Fuck you!"

His face flushed. "And none of that language, either. For God's sake, you're fourteen years old and you're dressing like a whore, cursing like a sailor and screwing around with a guy way too old for you."

Tears filled her eyes and she said, "You killed

him. You killed Birch."

"The guy was a piece of shit. If you live through this, don't get mixed up with a dick like that again. Only a pervert would mess with a girl your age."

This psycho was giving her *advice*? He had to be insane. Of course, kidnapping her and murdering Birch were the first clues of that. She hated to think what else he might have planned.

****

Abby called Diane from the truck.

"Abby, I was so worried!" Diane cried. "I've been trying to call you for two days. You didn't do the tours. I've had customers calling. You wouldn't answer your phone or your door. I was about ready to call the police."

Abby had decided to suspend the tours for now. Maybe for a lifetime if...

She shook her head. She wouldn't think that way. This nightmare would be over soon. She had to believe that. In the meantime, she'd shut down her excursions. What else could she do? Provide a disclaimer warning passengers that their tour guide could detonate at any moment?

"I'm fine," she told Diane. "But there's something Wil and I need to talk to you about. Can we come by?"

"Of course. What's going on? Where have you been?"

"I'll explain everything when I get there," Abby promised.

A few minutes later, they arrived at Diane's house. She lived in a cream-colored bungalow in a quiet neighborhood with neatly trimmed lawns. Before Abby and Wil had fully exited the pickup, Diane flung her front door open and dashed out to meet them. She took Abby in a fierce hug. Abby gasped, the incision in her abdomen sending shock waves of pain through her body, but Diane didn't seem to notice.

"I'm so glad you're okay," Diane said, releasing Abby. "Come in and tell me what happened."

Perry was sitting in the recliner and stood when they entered. "Hey, buddy." He reached out and shook Wil's hand, then looked at Abby. "You okay, hon? Diane's been going crazy."

"I'm okay," Abby said, and once she and Wil were seated on Diane's sofa, Abby began telling the story they'd decided on. "After you took me home, someone broke into my house and kidnapped me."

Diane's face paled. "What? Good God. Kidnapped? Are you okay?"

"I'm fine. He let me go, although we have no idea why. We're trying to figure out who he is and why he did this."

"Jesus." Perry sat forward. "Are you sure you're all right?"

Abby nodded and Diane said, "He didn't...rape you or anything, did he?"

Diane's expression was unreadable. There was concern there, but something different Abby couldn't identify. Shaking her head, Abby said, "No, nothing like that. I have no idea why he took me, what he wanted."

"Abby doesn't remember a lot about the evening you two went out," Wil interjected. "We were hoping you could answer some questions."

"We never should have left them," Perry said harshly. "They could have been..." He sighed and shook his head. "There are some sick bastards out there."

"I know," Wil agreed. "You'd think the local hangout in Blue Harbor would be safe."

"Everything seemed fine. No one threatening that I noticed," Diane said. "You know, it was really strange. Abby had some drinks, but not enough to get that wasted, then suddenly, she was...like...gone.

I had to help her to the car, help her into bed, the whole bit."

Wil slid to the edge of the sofa and withdrew a small notebook and pen from his shirt pocket. "Did anyone send a drink over?"

Diane gave a small smile and glanced apologetically at Abby. "Several men sent drinks over. Abby was quite popular that night."

Abby's face flushed and she didn't dare look at Wil.

His voice sounded unaffected as he continued, "Think carefully. Were all of the drinks brought over by the waitress or did anyone deliver them personally?"

Diane knitted her brow. "Most of them were brought over by the waitress, but that one guy, Matt. He hand-carried a couple of rounds. Then, another guy, I don't remember his name, brought us a drink." Her scowl deepened. "That was way early, though, so if he'd put something in it, I'm sure she'd have felt the effects sooner."

Wil nodded. "Was there anyone that paid special attention to Abby? Anyone who gave you the creeps?"

Slowly, Diane shook her head. "No. It was pretty much a normal night for two hot, sexy women out on the town." She attempted a feeble grin but Abby didn't smile back.

"I don't remember much at all," Abby said quietly, ashamed she'd been so out of it she hadn't known what was going on. "I can't believe I drank that much."

"It's not your fault," Wil assured her. "I bet someone slipped something, maybe Rohypnol, in your drink." A muscle clenched in his jaw and his hazel eyes hardened, darkening to a deep green. "And I think I know who it might have been."

"Matt?" Abby asked. When she'd mentioned him

to Wil earlier, Wil had told her a little about their history. Judging from the things her abductor had said, he had a long standing grudge against Wil, so it could possibly have been Matt.

Wil nodded. "I'll go talk to him and, even though it might be uncomfortable for you, I'd like for you to go with me. In spite of the kidnapper disguising his voice and appearance, you might recognize something that will confirm it was Matt."

Abby nodded, then turned to Diane. "Thanks," she told her. "For the information and for taking care of me that night."

Diane's eyes welled with tears and she swiped at them with quick, angry motions. "I didn't take care of you. I left you alone and some monster abducted you. I feel awful."

"It wasn't your fault." Abby stood and hugged her friend. "And don't worry, I'm fine."

She felt bad at deceiving Diane. Abby was anything but fine. But Wil's little girl was the one who was the most vulnerable. The one they had to save.

The one in the hands of a madman.

****

When they arrived back at Wil's house, he opened the front door for Abby. Her walk was tentative, careful. He saw her face blanch and clench with pain, just like he'd noticed at Diane's. She hadn't said anything, but he could see she was hurting.

"I'll go meet with Matt," he told her. "You stay here and rest."

Abby shook her head. "I need to be there. I need to see if he's the one, if I recognize him as the kidnapper."

"Fine." Wil sighed. "But we'll do it tomorrow. His office is closed and he probably wouldn't see me if I went to his house. He can't very well refuse if I show up at his office."

"Okay."

They'd already agreed Abby would stay at Wil's house, but when it came time to go to bed, she protested. "Wil, I think I should go home. I can't be around you, around anyone. I'm...dangerous," she finished in a tormented whisper.

He took her by the shoulders and looked into her eyes, trying to convey his determination, his concern about her.

"You're not dangerous. You're a victim. And you're in this mess because of me. I want you here, where I can keep an eye on you." He gave her a reassuring smile. "You don't scare me, okay?"

Tears filled her eyes, but she nodded. "Okay."

"You take my bed. I'll sleep on the sofa."

"I can't do that. You need your rest. I'll take the sofa."

Exasperated, he shook his head. "Abby, please. Don't oppose me at every turn. I want you to have my bed, and really, I'm too exhausted to argue."

She nodded again and they said goodnight. Wil watched her make her way down the hall. He listened as she ran water in the bathroom. He waited until the other settling down night noises had stopped and all he could hear was the wind moaning softly outside the windows.

He lay down on the sofa but couldn't sleep, couldn't close his eyes without seeing Lindsey, and couldn't lose himself in sleep without feeling guilty that she wasn't in her own bed.

After a few minutes, he heard Abby moving around in his room and knew she couldn't sleep either. He wanted to go to her, but didn't think it was a good idea. His desire to be with her wasn't all sexual, although admittedly that was a part of it. He mostly just felt the need to hold her.

He decided on a compromise, a prudent, safer

course of action.

He walked to his bedroom door, and tapped softly on it. "Abby," he spoke quietly. "Are you okay?"

"I'm fine," she replied through the barrier, but her voice sounded weak, frightened.

He put his hand on the doorknob but let it drop. Leaning his forehead against the smooth wood, he ran his fingertips down it. He stood there for several seconds, then, with a heavy sigh, made his way back to the living room.

The house smelled of Lindsey. Of her young girl lotions and perfumes and it made him ache. Wherever she was, he prayed she was all right. That she was not too frightened and that she had faith he'd bring her home, even though he wasn't sure *he* did.

He'd checked in with the station often, probably more often than he should have. He was sure he was driving them crazy. The entire force was searching for Lindsey and had promised to let him know as soon as they learned anything.

He dropped onto the sofa and flipped on the television, leaving it on mute so it wouldn't disturb Abby. A late night celebrity talk show was on. The people on the screen with their smiling faces taunted him. He resented them, these lucky souls whose children had not been kidnapped...whose loved ones had not been impregnated with a bomb.

Disgusted with them and himself, he hit the power button and watched the screen go black. He should do something constructive with the long hours that stretched before him, but all he could manage was to futilely mull over the situation. The sorrow and fear of not having his daughter home, safe in her bed, threatened to overwhelm him.

He knew he needed sleep but he hadn't been able to since Lindsey had disappeared. Remembering the sleeping pills the doctor had given him after Tara died, he considered taking one. Would they still be good after four years? He'd taken them for a few nights right after it happened. Then, one night, he hadn't heard Lindsey scream for him and by the time he'd reached her she was shaking and sobbing uncontrollably. He'd never taken them again.

He wouldn't take them now. What if he took them tonight and Lindsey needed him?

Scrubbing a hand over his eyes, he leaned his head back, checking the wall clock out of the corner of his eye. Jesus. Time was crawling along, excruciatingly, painfully dragging by.

His eyes drifted shut, then snapped open when his cell phone rang. It was three a.m. What the hell?

The readout said private, but even before he answered, Wil knew who it would be.

Chapter Nine

"Hello, Wil." The voice was disguised, and, just as Abby had said, it made him sound like Darth Vader. "I didn't wake you, did I?"

"No."

"Couldn't sleep, huh? That's too bad. Your little girl is sleeping like a baby."

Wil couldn't reply for a moment. He felt as if an invisible rubber band were around his throat, squeezing. The sensation moved up to his head and anger made his whole body tremble, hot with the need to hurt this bastard. "What have you done to her?" he finally managed in a voice as unrecognizable as the one on the other end of the line.

"Other than the obvious?" Even through the distortion, Wil detected amusement in the tone. "Don't worry. I haven't hurt her, physically or sexually. My tastes don't run to children. I may be a lot of things, but I'm not a pedophile."

"Let me talk to my daughter."

"No."

"I have to know she's okay. How do I know you haven't already—"

"Want me to make her scream?" The voice interrupted.

"No!"

"Then I guess you'll have to take my word for it."

"What do you want?"

"That's not the question you should be asking. The question you should be asking is, *why* do I want it?"

"Okay. Why do you want it?"

"You'll have to figure that out on your own, but maybe I can help you. What's the worst thing you've done? The thing you're most ashamed of?"

"The worst thing I've done?" Wil sighed in exasperation. "What the hell are you talking about?"

"You heard me. What is the worst thing, in your entire sorry life, that you've ever done?"

"Well," Wil said slowly. "I once rooted for the Yankees."

"You think this is funny, motherfucker? You think it's a *game*? I'm not the person you want to piss off, got it?"

"Yes. I'm sorry," Wil said quickly. "It won't happen again. Just tell me what you want."

"You'll find out soon enough. In the meantime, enjoy my little gift. Have you fucked her yet? I bet it was exciting, wasn't it? I mean, knowing at any time, she could go kaboom! Takes sex to a whole new level, gives a whole new meaning to the term 'banging'." The creepy voice guffawed loudly in Wil's ear, making his skin tighten. He wanted to fire down on him, wanted to threaten him and curse his black soul to hell. But he had to stay calm. For Lindsey. "I'll be in touch," the voice said before disconnecting the call.

Wil sat in the darkness for a long time after, until the sun rose, bringing rays of lemon-colored light into the room.

The worst thing you've ever done.

The worst thing he'd ever done was to let Tara die.

That made him more convinced than ever that Matt was behind this.

****

Matt Bingham was an attorney with an impressive office, and an even more impressive secretary. The office was all dark woods and crystal vases and leather furniture. The secretary was tall and gorgeous with platinum blonde hair and a powder blue clingy dress that was at the same time classy and alluring. When she informed Matt over the intercom that Wil and Abby were there to see him, he told her to send them in.

Bingham was less than friendly when he offered them a seat, although the smile he bestowed upon Abby dripped with smarmy charm.

"My time is limited," he said as soon as they were seated. "So I can only spare you a few moments. What can I do for you?"

Wil tamped down his dislike of the man and said, "I'd like to ask you a few questions about Friday night."

"What about it?"

"You took Abby and her friend, Diane, some drinks, I understand."

"Yes," Matt agreed slowly.

"Abby felt unwell later that evening. As a matter of fact, she was so out of it, someone managed to break into her house and kidnap her."

Bingham raised his eyebrows, his gaze shooting to Abby. "Kidnapped you? For God's sake, are you okay? How did you get away?"

She shrugged, keeping to the story they'd told Diane. "He didn't hurt me and for some reason, he let me go."

"Did you recognize him?"

Before Abby could answer, Wil cut in. "Why

would you ask that?"

Matt gave him a sardonic look. "I would think it might be easier to catch the guy if she knew who he was."

"He was disguised," Abby said. "His voice and his face."

Matt blew out a breath. "Damn." His eyes narrowed. "But that may mean you know the guy. He probably disguised himself to keep you from recognizing him, right?"

Wil answered for her. "Possibly, or since he intended to let her go, he didn't want her to ID him later."

"Look, I'm sorry I can't help you," Matt said. "But I know nothing about this. And I'm sure you're aware I don't have to speak with you. For one, you're not a cop, for another, I'm not being charged with anything." His stare was challenging. "Or am I?"

Wil held his gaze for a moment, then shook his head. "Right now, we're just gathering information."

"You've gathered all the information you can here. I'd like you to leave."

Even though he and Abby had agreed to stick with the story they'd told Diane, Wil decided to check Bingham's reaction, see if the man could produce the same amount of shock he had before.

"Lindsey's missing, too. We think the man who kidnapped Abby may have her."

This time, Matt actually gasped and his skin lightened a few shades. "Lindsey? How long has she been missing? Could she just be off with her friends?"

His shock seemed genuine. Had he not read about it in the papers? It had happened too late to be in the Sunday paper and Wil hadn't checked this morning's, but he would bet it was in there. "No. She was kidnapped and the boy who was with her at the time was found dead."

Matt pinched his nose between his thumb and forefinger and squeezed his eyes shut. "Poor thing. God." His eyes opened and they seemed to hold sincere concern. "I hope you find her. I hope she's okay."

"Thanks," Wil said grudgingly. He stood and Abby did the same. "I'll be in touch, Bingham. If you think of anything, give me a call. For your own sake."

Something in Bingham's face shifted. He'd read the threat and didn't like it. "I'm not holding anything back. Don't expect to hear from me."

"Okay." Wil shrugged casually. "But Abby's captor made it clear he had a score to settle with me. So, I figure it's someone who thinks I've wronged them. You can understand why you came to mind."

Bingham's face reddened. It was as if he'd had a thin string holding onto his control, and the string snapped.

"Are you accusing me of something? Because, if you are, I'll have your ass in a sling so fast you won't know what hit you." He came around the desk but kept his distance from Wil, his fists clenched against his sides. "Yes, I hate you, but I'm not a low-life criminal. I wouldn't go after Abby or Lindsey to get to you." His eyes glazed over and for a second, Wil thought he was going to cry. "You took Tara, let her die, robbed her of her life, but I would never hurt Lindsey. She's Tara's daughter and there was a time I hoped..." His voice trailed off and the fight seemed to leave him as he finished quietly, "...hoped she'd be mine." At the look on Wil's face, Matt said, "No, she couldn't have been. I never slept with Tara. I meant that I *wanted* to be Lindsey's father. Wanted to be with Tara and wanted you out of the picture. I think Tara eventually would have divorced you and married me. She wasn't happy with you, you know."

"Yeah? Was her suicide the first indication?"

Matt lifted his chin, glaring hostility at Wil, but didn't answer.

Wil tossed a business card on Matt's desk. "Give me a call if you think of anything."

They left the office building and stopped just outside the door. Abby touched Wil's arm and searched his face. "Are you okay?"

Standing on the sidewalk, Wil watched the cars whiz by, the pedestrians passing them. A plump woman pushing a toddler in a stroller glanced at them and smiled.

Keep an eye on your baby, Wil told her silently, *don't ever let her out of your sight.*

"Wil?" Abby repeated. "Are you okay?"

Wil nodded. "Yeah," he said tightly.

"Hearing he was in love with your wife couldn't have been easy."

Wil shrugged. "I've known it for years. All I'm concerned about now is whether he had anything to do with Lindsey's disappearance."

"What does your gut tell you?"

"I don't know. My gut hasn't been normal since Lindsey was taken." One corner of his mouth lifted in a humorless smile. "Actually, since you ended things between us."

"I'm sorry, Wil. I didn't want to do that, but—"

"No. You were right. You wanted to avoid conflict. Wanted peace. You can't have that as long as you're involved with me. I think what's happening now pretty emphatically confirms that."

"It's not your fault."

"No?" Wil gave a derisive snort of laughter. He turned to Abby and gripped her upper arms, pulling her close, heedless of the fact they were in public and might draw attention. "A fucking lunatic planted a *bomb* inside your body to get back at me. So, in what possible way, on what fucking planet, could this not be my fault? Huh? Can you tell me that?"

"Let me go," Abby said through gritted teeth.

"First, you have to tell me how the *fuck* it's not my fault."

"Okay, fine," Abby hissed. "It *is* your fault. Do you feel better now? I mean, even though you don't know what you did to piss this guy off, obviously you did something. Maybe you cut him off in traffic, or fucked his girlfriend, or stole his hot wheels in grade school. I don't know and neither do you. But that's not the important thing. What we need to worry about is getting this goddamned thing out of me and finding your daughter. So why don't you quit being a dick and let's figure out a way to do that!"

As quickly as it came, the fight went out of him, and all he felt was hollow and ashamed. "Christ, Abby. I'm sorry.

She nodded and pulled free, silently making her way to the truck.

Once they were both seated in the cab, Wil sat staring out the windshield, not starting the engine.

"Did Matt's voice sound familiar?" he asked. "I know the kidnapper used a voice box, but when you were outside the motel room, it was his real voice, right?"

Abby nodded. "Yes, but as I said, it still sounded like he was trying to disguise it. It seemed a little high-pitched, unnatural. It didn't sound at all like Matt Bingham."

"What about his height? Does that match?"

She blew out a breath. "I'm sorry, but I'm not sure. I was in shock, drugged. My perception was off. It seems like he was a little taller than Matt, but I just can't be sure."

"It's okay." He tapped on the steering wheel for a few seconds, then said, "You think you can find that motel?"

"I doubt it. I was unconscious on the way there

and blindfolded on the way back."

"Do you know about how long it took you to get to where he dropped you off?"

"It seemed like forever, but I'd say probably fifteen or twenty minutes."

"There's water on one side of town, and east of here is residential. Only a few areas that have motels within fifteen or twenty minutes of here. It wasn't a nice motel, right?"

"No. It was a bit seedy."

"The motels west of here are seedy. We'll head that direction. Might get lucky."

****

They found the correct one on the third attempt.

At each motel, they asked to see the rooms. One manager let them in at no charge. At the second one, they had to pay for a night. But neither of the room setups looked familiar to Abby.

The third motel was called 'Pelican Cove', its name lending a more pleasant ambiance than it actually provided. The clerk, Gerald according to his name tag, was a short, thin man with close-set eyes. His hair was dyed black and his stained tan pants were belted just below his rib cage.

Gerald made them pay, but this motel rented by the hour, so it didn't cost much to look.

Abby knew it was the right one as soon as she stepped through the door. The décor was a little different. The other drapes had been one solid color, sort of a dirty butterscotch. These were the same shade, but also had blue vertical stripes running through them. Where the other carpet had been dark brown, this was a dusky blue.

She raised her gaze to the ceiling. The water stains were different, too. She'd stared at the others enough that she was certain she would be able to identify their pattern. She dragged her gaze to the bed. Yes. The metal headboard and dingy leaf-patterned bedspread were the same.

Your life, and those around you, depends on your lover. He holds your fate in his hands.

She felt trembles start from deep within, traveling up through her stomach and into her arms and legs.

She walked slowly to the bathroom and saw the cracked vinyl shower curtain, so much like the one that had stood between her and the glittering eyes of—

"Abby?"

She let out a small yelp and whirled to find Wil standing behind her. She hadn't heard him approach.

"This is it," she told him breathlessly as a film of sweat broke out over her skin. "This is where he held me."

"Come here," he said, and pulled her into his arms. Holding her gently, he stroked her hair, murmuring reassurances until the trembles stopped.

After a while, he released her and brushed the damp hair back from her face. "Let's get out of here," he said.

They went back to the manager's office, and Wil said to the clerk, "We'll need to look at your registrations for this past weekend."

The guy shook his head. "Sorry, can't let you do that. Private."

Wil leaned on the counter, so close he could have whispered in the guy's hairy ear.

"I'm gonna do you a favor," Wil told him in a cool, controlled voice. "I'll look at them, look at just those few days. Just me. I won't have the sheriff's department issue a warrant for all your records. I won't have the cops methodically and thoroughly examine all your documents. I won't have them upset your regular customers and most likely find something that would earn you a few years in the pen." He smiled benignly. "Because that's just the sort of nice fellow I am."

The guy swallowed hard, his Adam's apple working up and down. "Hold on a second."

He bent under the counter and Abby tensed, thinking he might come up with a shotgun, but when he rose, he held a large, bound book in his hands. He slammed it on the counter and opened it, flipping pages. He found what he wanted and turned it around for Wil to read.

Wil was silent as his gaze scanned the page. He took out a notebook and wrote a list of names, then pushed the log book back across the counter.

He and Abby left and when they were in the truck, Wil shook his head. "Nothing on the list raised any flags." He passed the notebook to her. "You might take a look."

She did but also didn't recognize any names. "I'm sure he used an alias."

"Yeah. But I figured it wouldn't hurt to try." Wil's phone rang and he listened for a moment, then said, "No shit? Who is it? Okay, we'll be right there."

"What?" Abby asked.

"They have a suspect. Ray wants you to come in and see if you can ID him. Or the mask."

Chapter Ten

The suspect in Ray's office claimed his name was Jesus Christ, and he was a carpenter from Galilee.

Wil didn't believe him because he didn't think Jesus would have been wearing dirty thermal underwear pants with a Jeff Gordon Nascar T-shirt, or that he would smell like body odor and stale urine.

Beach patrol had picked Jesus up for panhandling. When they ran a check, they found out his AKA was Harris Thompson and he'd been hauled in several times before. This time, he had a hockey mask in his possession. He claimed he'd found it in a trash can along the pier.

"When did you find the mask? Where was the trash can located? Did you notice anything else of interest in the same can? Where were you on Saturday evening between the hours of midnight and six a.m.? Was anyone with you?"

Ray fired the questions at the transient and most were answered with incoherent, nonsensical responses.

Wil stepped outside the office and went to

Abby's side, where she watched through the glass window.

"What do you think?" Wil asked.

She wrinkled her nose and shook her head. "No way. For one, I don't think he's fit for such an undertaking. But mainly I don't think it was him because I would most definitely have remembered that smell."

"Yeah. He's not our guy."

"Wil?" a voice said behind them.

Abby and Wil turned and saw Mayor Micah Bingham heading toward them, flanked by a middle-aged blonde woman in a power suit, and a frail looking, bespectacled man. The two of them held back as Micah approached.

Tall and John Wayne rugged, Micah had dark hair lightly dusted with gray and his face was tanned from many hours on the golf course. He patted Wil on both shoulders, squeezing before he dropped his hands. "I'm so sorry about Lindsey. Don't worry, they'll find her. She'll be fine."

Wil nodded. "Thanks."

Micah turned to Abby and reached out to take her hands in his. "You must be Abigail."

She nodded. "Abby Bishop. Nice to meet you, Mr. Mayor."

"Please. Call me Micah." He gave her a white-toothed smile and, still holding Abby's hands, he looked at Wil. "I heard you talked to Matthew. You don't really think he's involved, do you?"

"We're speaking with anyone who might have been in the bar that night," Wil responded noncommittally.

"Of course. I don't believe Matt would do something like this, but if I find out he knows anything about it..." Micah shook his head. "Well, let's just say I'll make sure he regrets it." He nodded through the window toward Thompson. "I heard they had a suspect. Heard you were here at the station and I wanted to come down and offer my support. Anything you need, buddy, anything at all, you give a yell. We'll get this bastard."

"Thanks," Wil said again.

Ray came out of the office and he and the mayor exchanged greetings.

"Listen," Micah said. "I'll get out of your way and let you get down to the business of finding your little girl. Remember, if there's anything at all I can do..."

Wil nodded and Micah clasped him on the shoulder affectionately, then left, taking his mini-entourage with him.

"I think we all agree this ain't our guy," Ray said to Wil once the mayor was gone. "Want us to hold him for a bit or let him loose?"

"No need to hold him," Wil admitted reluctantly. "As you said, not our guy. Of course, we'll want to get DNA from the mask."

Ray nodded. "Yeah, we're on it. But if we can't get anything to compare it to, won't do much good."

Wil blew out a breath and nodded slowly. "Won't do a damned bit of good." His phone rang and he looked at the caller ID. Another unfamiliar number. A cold wave of anticipation and anxiety washed over him.

"Yes?" he said into the mouthpiece.

"Time's running out, Willie boy. Did you figure it out yet?"

Wil switched to speaker phone so the sheriff could listen in. Maybe something the guy said would provide some kind of clue.

They'd already tried to trace the cell phone signal, but a different phone had been used each time and the locations were scattered. There was nothing to indicate exactly where he was calling from.

"I want my daughter back," Wil said tightly.

"People in hell want ice water. You give me what I want and I'll think about giving you what you want. Eventually."

"I don't know what the fuck you want," Wil said, barely holding onto his sanity as he bit out the words.

"Give Abby a message for me. Tell her she should thank me. At least her womb's no longer empty."

Wil looked at Abby and saw the color leach from her face. She held her fingertips to her lips and tears swam in her eyes.

"What the hell is that supposed to mean?" Wil ground out.

"Ask her what it means. I bet there are all sorts of things you don't know about your pretty girlfriend." A gruff chuckle traveled from the speaker. "Gotta go. Think about what I said. Think hard, Teddy. You really need to come up with some answers...and soon."

The call disconnected and Wil nearly shook with rage. He wanted to lash out at something, at someone, but the person his anger was directed at was unreachable.

"You want me to deputize you?" Ray asked. "That way, you can really get involved in the case."

What Wil had to do to catch this bastard might not exactly follow the law. He took a deep breath and said, "No. I want you to accept my resignation."

****

Abby kept playing the words over and over in her head. *At least her womb's no longer empty.* He knew. The bastard knew about the baby.

"...not sure what to do next."

"Huh?" She hadn't realized Wil was speaking. They'd left the sheriff's department and were sitting in a coffee shop on main street. She barely remembered getting there, or ordering the cup of warm latté her hands now gripped like a lifeline.

"I'm at a dead end. I don't know what to do, where to look next. The son of a bitch is toying with me."

Abby barely nodded. Her heart lay like a heavy stone in her chest. She hadn't told anyone her secret except Diane. She wasn't sure why she'd trusted the truth to her, maybe because Diane had been her only friend. Wil had a right to know. She didn't know why she hadn't trusted him with it before. Maybe because it was just too painful to share, too much of a door to her soul.

"I was pregnant," she whispered.

Wil's eyebrows rose, but he didn't comment. He reached out and took her wrist in his warm grip.

"We were attacked, my husband and I. They broke into our house. Threw me down the stairs." She drew in a shaky breath. "I lost the baby."

"God, I'm sorry. I had no idea."

Abby shrugged. "I don't like to talk about it."

Wil nodded. "Maybe not, but don't you think it's time?"

He was probably right, but she couldn't say any more. She hadn't even told Diane all of it. Not the details, not the entire horrific truth. It was something Abby couldn't stand to think about, let alone say aloud. She'd been touched by violence. No, not touched, seared. Branded so deeply she was amazed the scars weren't visible to the naked eye. She couldn't share any more with Wil than she already had.

Abby shook her head and took a sip of the cooling latté. "Can we not talk about this any more, please? I just wanted you to know why he said what he did. But, how on earth could he know about the miscarriage? It happened six years ago in Michigan. How could he know?"

"You haven't told anyone?"

She didn't respond at first. Finally, she sighed and shrugged. "I told Diane."

****

Wil pulled the pickup in front of Diane's house and parked.

Abby had wanted to come, but he'd told her it was best he speak with Diane alone. He didn't know how...persistent...he might need to be. He wouldn't hurt Diane, but if he thought she was lying, he wasn't beyond using a little intimidation.

Perry's Firebird, top down, was in the driveway. When Wil knocked on the door, Diane opened it, wearing a robe.

"Wil, hello." Her voice was friendly enough but held an underlying tone of unwelcome. "What are you doing here? Did you try to call?"

"No. I was in the neighborhood and I wanted to ask you something, so I stopped by. Is this a bad time?"

She hesitated, then stepped back to let him in. "No. I was just getting in the shower, but I have a few minutes."

He stepped into the living room and looked around. "Isn't Perry here?"

"Yes, but he's still asleep."

"I see. He spent the night?"

She nodded slowly. "Yes, why?"

Wil shrugged. "No reason, just asking. Listen, I need to know if you told anyone else what Abby told you about her miscarriage."

Diane's eyes rounded slightly, then dropped away from Wil's. "No, no one."

"No one? Not even Perry?"

"No. Not even Perry. Girlfriends don't tell one another's secrets, not even to their boyfriends. I wouldn't betray Abby like that."

"Abby said you're the only one she told. That no

one else in Blue Harbor knows."

"Yeah, so?"

"It seems there may be someone else who found out. I'm just trying to figure out how."

Diane shrugged. "I'm sorry. I can't help you."

Wil let out a frustrated breath. "Diane, if you're hiding something that could help catch this guy..."

She gave a quick shake of her head. "I wouldn't do that, Wil. I want you to find him as badly as anyone."

There was something about her that didn't quite feel right. It was a tone, maybe her body language, maybe the way she wouldn't meet his eyes. He couldn't quite put his finger on it, but there was something.

"Okay. Thanks." He stepped back out onto the porch. "If you think of anything, anything at all, give me a call."

"I will. Trust me. I want to do whatever I can to help."

Wil nodded and climbed back into his pickup. That intangible little something kept niggling at his mind as he pulled out of Diane's neighborhood.

Diane had seemed just a little furtive. Like she'd been caught off guard or something. But that wasn't it. It was... What?

He gave a frustrated shake of his head. Jesus. He was sleep-deprived and stressed to the max. He couldn't think straight.

Ten minutes or so later, while sitting behind a white Camry at a red light, it hit him.

"Shit." He looked behind him and slapped the steering wheel in frustration. A car in front and a car behind.

He hit the horn but nothing happened. Of course not. Did he think the Camry would run a red light because he honked?

Finally, the light changed and the car moved

just enough for him to make a u-turn, earning the angry blast of several horns.

He sped back to Diane's. The driveway was empty. He ran up onto the porch and banged his fist against the door.

Diane opened it, still wearing a robe. Her eyes widened. "What is it?"

"Where is he?"

"Who?"

"You know who. Perry."

"He left."

"But he stayed here all night?"

"Yes."

"And he was asleep when I was here a few minutes ago, but he's already awake *and* gone?"

She shifted from one foot to the other and pulled her robe more tightly around her. "Yes. Why?"

Wil leaned forward until his nose was centimeters from hers. "Perry never leaves the top down on his car, not if he's going to be away from it for more than sixty seconds." His jaw clenched as anger built inside him. "Damned sure not overnight."

She flinched and shook her head. "What are you saying?"

"I'm saying Perry didn't spend the night. He wouldn't leave his baby unprotected for that long. I'm saying you're lying. What do you know about my daughter's disappearance and what happened to Abby?"

"I don't know anything about it," she said, but her eyes slid away from him and he knew she was lying.

"Where's your boyfriend?"

"I don't know," she shouted and now there was a hint of tears and defiance in her voice.

"You're lying to me, Diane. I don't know what the fuck is going on, but I know you're lying."

"Get out," she screamed. "Get the hell out of my house!"

"I'm going. But you're coming with me."

"Where?"

"To the police department. The sheriff's going to want to talk to you."

"I'm not going anywhere with you. You can't make me," she added petulantly.

Wil gripped her upper arm and squeezed. "You're going with me. You can either get dressed while I wait, or you can go in your robe. But I promise, one way or another, you're going."

She lifted her chin and stared him in the eye for a few moments, her lips trembling and tears spilling down her cheeks. Finally, she said, "Let me go and I'll get dressed."

Chapter Eleven

Wil leaned with one hand on the two-way mirror of the interrogation room. Diane had been in there for two hours and hadn't cracked. Wil hadn't questioned her—he wasn't part of the force—but he'd watched.

Cuddly, lovable Ray had played bad cop to Lesli's sympathetic 'us women have to stick together' good cop routine. Nothing had worked. Ray was now leaning toward Diane, invading her space, scowling and speaking rapidly. Diane shrank away from him but didn't respond.

The sheriff shoved back his chair and stormed from the room, slamming the door behind him. He stalked over to Wil, his demeanor doing a one-eighty when he spoke. "She's not gonna budge."

"Looks that way," Wil agreed.

"I told her we could hold her for forty-eight without charging her and she didn't even blink. What do you think we should do?"

Wil raised his eyebrows. "You're asking me how to handle the case?"

"I'm asking you as a friend and a former cop whose record says you know your shit. And, as

Lindsey's father. So, what do you want me to do?"

"Let her go."

"Yeah?"

"Yeah. She'll most likely be in contact with Perry and she might lead us to him."

"Want me to put a tail on her?"

Wil shook his head. "No tail. I'll keep an eye on her."

****

After Diane was released, Wil followed her home, parking a few houses down.

He called Abby.

"How's it going with Diane?" she asked.

"I'm positive she knows more than she's telling us and I have a strong feeling Perry's involved."

"Perry? Why do you think that?"

"How many other people would Diane have told about your miscarriage? And, she lied to me this morning about how long Perry had been at her house."

"Why would Perry do something like this to you?"

"I can't imagine. But I can't imagine why anyone else would, either. The department's running a background check on them both."

"But, she's my friend and Perry's your friend. Surely they wouldn't do something so awful."

"Micah and Ray are my friends. Perry was more of a buddy. Guys are different about that stuff. We didn't get as close as you and Diane."

"I don't know. I've known her less than a year. I guess you never *really* know people."

"Actually, I was hoping you could tell me what you do know about her. It seems the two of you confided in one another. Maybe she told you something that will help us?"

"I don't know," Abby said softly, "If I really thought she was behind this... But she trusted me, took me in her confidence. It seems like a betrayal."

"I understand. But it appears she told someone *your* secret. If she *is* involved in what's happening, she's done far worse than betray you. Yours and Lindsey's lives are hanging in the balance. I'd say breaking a confidence is minor in light of that. Anything you can tell me might help. Something about her family, background, maybe even a crime she's committed."

There was silence on the other end, then Abby said, "She has a child."

"What?"

"She and Perry had a daughter, but Diane gave her up for adoption. She didn't want to, but Perry insisted. Diane said she's regretted it ever since. She sees the girl a few times a year, but the child doesn't know Diane is her mother. It's an agreement she made with the adoptive parents. If Diane ever tells the girl who she is, the parents will cut off all contact forever. That would absolutely crush Diane."

Wil's heart sped up. This could be something. "I need you to tell me everything you can about this girl. Where she lives, her age, name, everything."

Abby gave a small sigh of resignation and then she told him.

Wil called Ray and asked him to send someone to take over surveillance. When Prescott arrived, Wil drove to the police department and by the time he left there, he had a print-out on twelve-year-old Brittany Goddard and was headed to Crowley, Florida, a small town eighty-five miles east of Blue Harbor.

It was close to nine p.m. when Wil pulled into the upper middle class neighborhood on the edge of Crowley. The Goddard's lived in a large, red brick, single-story house with a carefully landscaped lawn and a two-car garage.

Since Brittany was an only child, it didn't take

long for Wil to locate her bedroom through the binoculars. Her room was the one with the fire department sticker on the window, letting firemen know which room held a child so they could rescue the child first. Not as much of a safety precaution as one might think. Not if you took kidnappers and pedophiles into consideration.

Wil waited until late that night when he was relatively certain the occupants of the house were asleep. Then he made his way to Brittany's window.

Using a glasscutter, he cut out a hole just large enough to slip his pen light through and to give him a little wiggle room. Had the pink curtains been open, he wouldn't have had to make the hole. He made a mental note to anonymously inform Brittany's parents that they needed to replace her window.

Slipping the pen light through the opening in the glass, he pulled the curtain back and let the beam play over the room. Against one wall was a brass daybed. A small figure lay under the comforter, facing the wall. Blonde hair spilled out over the pillow.

There was a chance the miniscule shine might wake the girl, but it was unlikely. If it did, Wil could be long gone before she alerted her parents.

He moved the light around, taking in the details of the girl's life. On the dresser stood a few softball trophies and a jewelry box. A couple of Dr. Pepper cans and some clothing were piled around them. A cloth-covered board hung on the wall, framed with a squiggly blue border. The board held a collage of celebrity photos that had been cut out of magazines.

Because Wil had a teenage daughter, he recognized Hillary Duff and Justin Timberlake, but none of the others. In the center of the pictures, beneath haphazardly placed red block letters that read 'Me and Cami', was a snapshot of two smiling girls, one blonde, one dark-haired, their cheeks pressed together as they posed for the camera.

Satisfied he'd seen enough, he clicked the pen light off and pulled it back through the hole.

The girl hadn't stirred.

****

Wil drove to Diane's house. Prescott's cruiser sat at the end of the block. Wil pulled up beside him and told him he'd take over the watch.

Once the patrol car was out of sight, Wil parked his pickup in front of the next door neighbor's house and moved stealthily to Diane's back yard. He jimmied the lock on her kitchen door, letting himself in. He sent up a brief prayer of thanks that there was no alarm.

Using the faint moonlight streaming in between the blinds, he found Diane's bedroom.

She lay sleeping, her body beneath the blankets rising and falling with her breaths. He sat in a chair next to her bed for ten minutes or so before she sensed him and bolted to a sitting position, a small scream leaving her as she clutched the covers to her chin. Her hair was wild, her eyes round with fear. A crease from the pillow marred her left cheek.

Her expression changed from fear to confusion and then to irritation when she recognized him. "Wil! What the hell are you doing here?"

"I thought I'd give you another chance to come clean about Perry."

She dropped the covers, revealing a blue flannel nightgown, and pointed at the door. "Get out, now! Before I call the cops."

"Sorry, sweetheart, I *am* the cops."

"You resigned."

He lifted one shoulder in a casual shrug. "Once a cop, always a cop. But that doesn't really matter right now. Hear me out, and if you still want to call the cops afterward, I'll let you." He leaned forward in the chair and linked his hands between his knees. "If you don't want to talk about Perry, how about if we talk about Brittany?"

Her face blanched and a small moan escaped her lips.

"I can tell by your reaction that you love your daughter as much as I love mine."

A look of resolve entered her eyes. "Abby told you I have a daughter? So what?"

"I'm trying to decide what to do with that information. I don't know whether to tell her the truth about you so Mike and Cassandra Goddard will never let you see her again, or make something..." He paused and gave her a level stare. "...*happen* to her. Maybe something like what happened to Lindsey."

Diane's lips stretched into a brittle smile. Her voice quivered when she spoke. "Just because you know her name, doesn't mean you can find *her*. Or get to her."

"No? Not even at one of her softball games? Or when she stays at Cami's? Or, maybe in her bedroom, where I could slip in and snatch her right out of her comfy day bed?"

With each word Wil spoke, Diane's face paled even more until it looked ghostly in the bedroom's dim light. "You're a cop," she said, her voice sounding strangled.

Wil leaned back in his chair and smiled. "Resigned, remember?"

"But...you're a father."

He nodded in agreement. "Yes, but I'm the father of a rebellious, high-maintenance, smartass teenage girl. You can imagine why the species doesn't elicit much sympathy in me."

She shook her head. "You wouldn't. I know you woul—"

He leapt from the chair and slammed his hands

on the headboard, one on each side of her trembling body, so close he could smell her perfume and the faint scent of garlic and booze.

"Whoever did this," he growled into her terrified face, "has fucked with the two people I love most in the world. I don't give a damn about anything *but* that right now. You see, I have nothing else to lose. I'm certain you know who it is. Certain enough that I'm willing to take my frustrations out on your little girl if you don't tell me what the fuck I need to know." He punctuated each of the last words by banging his fist on the headboard next to her face.

"Okay!" she screamed, sobbing and shaking her head wildly back and forth, her hands clamped tightly over her ears. "Okay, okay, okay. It's fucking Perry, okay? Please don't hurt my little girl."

Wil went limp and dropped back onto the chair, the adrenaline leaving him as if it had been siphoned with a hose. "Where is he and what has he done with my daughter?"

Diane's body shook and tears streaked down her cheeks. "I don't know. I swear. I don't know where he is or where he's holding Lindsey. But she's fine, I promise."

"Don't say her name," Wil growled. "Don't you ever say her fucking name."

Her eyes rounded and a fresh wave of tears filled them. "He didn't tell me where he has her. I swear."

"How do you get in touch with him?"

"I don't. He's not keeping his cell on and he has a supply of those throw away trac phones with different numbers. He calls me to check in periodically."

"When? How often?"

"He calls me in the mornings, usually around six or six-thirty."

Wil's gaze went to the clock, as did Diane's. Four

a.m. "He should call in a few hours, then."

"What do we do in the meantime?" Diane asked shakily.

Wil raked a hand through his hair and sighed wearily. "We wait."

He wanted to call Abby, but hopefully, she was asleep and, if she was, he didn't want to disturb her rest.

"For what it's worth," Diane said, tears making her voice thick. "I had no idea he'd hurt Lind—your daughter—or Abby. The night she and I went out, he told me to slip something in her drink, then take her home and he'd meet me there, do the rest. I did as he asked, but if I'd known his plan was to hurt her, I'd never have gone along with it. By the time I found out, I was in too deep."

"Just what *is* his plan?"

She shrugged. "I don't know exactly. He lets me know only what I need to know as we go along. He's been watching you for years. When you moved here, he followed you and when you started dating Abby, we insinuated ourselves in your lives."

"Why watch me for so long before making his move?"

"I don't know. He kept saying he needed to prepare, everything had to be just right. Befriending you and Abby was part of it. The thing is, I really grew to care about Abby, consider her a friend." She gave a choked laugh. "I know it sounds crazy, but sometimes I forgot being her friend was just part of the plan."

"Why is he doing this? Why does he hate me?"

"Because," she said, looking him square in the eye, "you murdered his sister."

Chapter Twelve

Wil stared at her incredulously. "I what?"

"You murdered his sister," Diane repeated. "I don't know all the details, but he said you killed her."

"That's crazy."

She shrugged. "That's what he said. It happened just before I met him. He and his sister were very close growing up. His parents were abusive alcoholics and treated him and his sister like shit. They had a huge life insurance on both kids. When Perry's sister died, they collected and lived like royalty for a little while. Then, they both died in a car accident. I always wondered if Perry..." She shrugged again. "But I can't say for sure. Anyway, Perry inherited all the money from his parents and he's made it his life's goal to avenge his sister. He adored her. He always talks about how smart she was. About how, in spite of her upbringing, Marissa would have made something of herself."

The name hit Wil like the gust of a hurricane. "Marissa? Did she and Perry have different last names?"

"Yes. Marissa was his half sister. Same mother,

different father. But they couldn't have been closer if they'd been full blood siblings."

"Oh Christ." Wil now knew why Perry hated him.

Thirteen years ago, in Miami, Wil had been called out on a liquor store robbery. The clerk had been shot to death. Wil and his partner, Rafe, had taken the call. Rafe was a rookie who'd only been on the force for six months.

They confronted the suspect leaving the store. It was dark, and they couldn't get a good look at the figure, but they could see a gun in the gloved hand. Their commands to drop the weapon were ignored. Rafe headed toward the suspect, gun pointed.

When Wil ordered his partner to fall back, shots rang out and Rafe dropped to the ground. The suspect swung the gun toward Wil and Wil fired his weapon.

It was afterward they discovered the suspect was a seventeen-year-old girl, Marissa Hoffman. She died before reaching the hospital.

Rafe survived but was paralyzed and hadn't been on the force long enough to earn much of a disability pension. He had a wife and two young children.

For years, Wil had questioned his actions. The thought of ending a young girl's life was almost more than he could bear. But, she'd murdered a sixty-five-year old man who owned the liquor store, and she'd ruined the life of a young police officer. Wil dealt with his guilt.

But now he understood why Perry hated him so much.

And how very precarious, how very serious, Lindsey's situation really was.

****

Wil was startled from a light sleep by the ringing of a phone. He was surprised he'd dozed, but a look at the clock told him it had only been a few minutes.

Diane stared at him as she picked up the receiver from the nightstand.

"Perry? You have to stop this. You have to let Lindsey go and end things now without anyone getting hurt. They know I'm involved somehow and it won't take long to figure out you're the one behind this." Moisture swam in her eyes. "They know about Brittany, and they're going to hurt her if you don't let Lindsey go." She listened for a few seconds. "Wil," she said, obviously responding to a query about who 'they' were. "Yes, he's serious. You didn't see the look on his face." Diane's eyes met Wil's and her voice dropped to a whisper. "I know he'll hurt my baby. I know it."

Diane listened for a bit more, then said, "You don't mean that. You can't be serious." Her face drained of what little color she had left and tears poured from her eyes. "No. No way! I won't let you—" Her face reddened, and her expression turned to rage. She said, "You piece of shit. Your revenge is more important than our daughter's life? Sorry motherfu—"

She stopped. Perry must have hung up. She closed the phone and her eyes were dead when she looked at Wil. "He said he wouldn't release Lindsey. He's willing to take the chance with Brittany's life. He said he doesn't even know her, but his sister was the person he loved most in this world."

Wil's heart sank with her words. Even though he now knew who had his daughter, finding him and stopping him were beginning to seem impossible.

****

The sliding door was opened a crack, just enough to let the evening breeze in and Abby breathed deeply of the clean air and ocean. She stared out through her own reflection in the glass, watching the moon play on the surface of the water.

Wil's image joined hers and she gave him a small smile.

"How you holding up?" he asked.

She shrugged, not turning around. "Okay. You?"

His gaze stared over her head into the blackness beyond the deck. "Wondering about Lindsey. Where she is. How she's doing. If she's scared. If she's hungry. If she thinks I'm not trying hard enough to find her." Even with the distortion of the glass, Abby saw a sheen of moisture in his eyes. "I don't think I ever told you, but she's afraid of the dark. Still, at fourteen, she has to sleep with a nightlight. If she has a friend over, she doesn't, she's too embarrassed. But any other time..." He drew in a long, shuddering breath. "I'm sure it's because of her mother. The bad dreams."

Abby turned to face him. "I'm so sorry, Wil."

He looked down at her, his eyes not really seeing her, their tormented expression far away, with his little girl. "She wanted a lamp left on her mother's grave, didn't want her spending eternity in the dark, alone. I got Tara one of those eternal flames and that seemed to placate Lindsey. I wonder if he's leaving a light on for her."

Abby stepped closer and slipped her arms around his waist, hugging him tightly. "It will be okay. We'll find her."

"You know," he said, and she felt the low rumble of his words against her ear where it rested on his chest. "When I was thinking of giving up police work, I was terrified. It's all I've ever done, all I've ever wanted to do. I kept asking myself, if I'm not a cop, then who am I? You know what made it possible for me to give it up?" She didn't answer. She didn't think he expected one. "When I realized who I was. I'm Lindsey's father, that's who." His voice lowered with the rasp of tears. "She's my world, Abby. I can't lose her."

Abby tightened her grip, holding him for several moments. She could feel their hearts beating in sync, keeping the same rhythm, reaching out to one another without words.

Finally, she pulled away. She expected to see tears when she looked into his face, but his eyes were dry. They were studying her with an intense look, seeming to reach deep inside her, into a part no one had ever touched.

Not even Chase.

Suddenly, she wanted to tell Wil about that night. Tell him everything. It was strange. Hers and Wil's relationship, or at least the romantic aspect of it, was over. But she felt closer to him than she ever had. It was a poignant, bittersweet connection, but it was there.

She walked over to the sofa, sank into the soft cushion, and waited until Wil was seated beside her to speak.

"My husband, Chase, was self-absorbed and uncaring," she said without preamble. "He cheated on me throughout our three-year marriage. I was ready to divorce him. Our marriage had been over for months, but we were still going through the motions. I was trying to figure out the right way to tell him I was leaving when I discovered I was pregnant." A deep, wrenching pain shafted through her heart at the memory. "I was going to abort it. I thought a baby would make it too difficult to divorce him. I never even told him I was pregnant."

Wil reached out and took her hand. "You don't have to tell me this if you don't want to."

As if he hadn't spoken, she continued. "Just before bedtime one night, there was a loud banging on the door. Chase opened it. He didn't even look through the peephole. We lived in a safe neighborhood. It never occurred to him that..." She shuddered and swallowed against the lump forming in her throat. "Three men forced their way in, wearing ski masks, carrying guns. They demanded our money and valuables. Chase led them upstairs, telling them they could have whatever they wanted, but to please not hurt me."

She shook her head, her mouth twisting into a wry, sad grin. "It was the only time in our marriage I remember him putting me first. One of the gunmen grabbed me by the arm, dragged me up the stairs behind the others. Once we reached the landing, he...he...touched me. He started to—"

She stopped, once again feeling his hot breath on her neck, smelling the repulsive odor of it and the cheap cologne he wore. "I fought him. I struggled and kicked, trying to break free. Chase saw what was happening and tried to help me, but the other men had him...they hit him..."

Her breath came in short gasps as she relived the horror. Wil tightened his hold but she was barely aware of it, barely aware of him at that moment. "I scratched my attacker's eyes and he hit me. I fell. Down the stairs. I landed, hard. I lay there, looking up at the horror above me." Tears flowed down her cheeks, her body cold and tight with the memories. "They beat him..."

She fell silent and Wil slid closer to her, placing a comforting arm around her shoulders and pulling her to his warmth. "You don't have to do this," he whispered hoarsely.

"They beat him. Then they shot him. He fell, face forward, his head hanging over the railing, looking at me," she ended, her voice as guttural and raw as if she'd been screaming for hours.

"Oh, God," Wil said. "I'm so sorry."

Abby couldn't tell him the other. Couldn't tell him how she'd been lying at the bottom of the stairs, feeling her baby leave her body as she looked up into her husband's pleading eyes. She'd wondered what he'd been pleading for. Forgiveness? For her to save him?

It didn't matter, because in the next moment, he was dead, and she couldn't give him what he asked for. The killers left then, taking whatever they could carry, for some reason leaving her alone and alive.

Later she was told she'd lain there for hours. She hadn't been aware of the passage of time. All awareness had been sucked into a black void. The only thing she could see, the only thing that was real to her, was her husband's eyes. She still saw them sometimes in her sleep.

"Now, I see," Wil said quietly. "I understand. You tried so hard to get away from violence and I've brought it right back to you."

Abby pulled away from him and stood, walking back to stare out the patio door. Her voice was mechanical as she replied, "Sometimes you can't hide. It will find you no matter what. Sometimes, you have to fight."

She heard Wil move, felt him stand behind her, met his eyes in the glass. He rubbed her shoulders gently, kneading out the tension. A slow, languorous warmth moved through her at his touch and she sighed, letting her head fall back.

They stood like that for several moments, his hands moving over her arms, softly, soothingly, then back up to her shoulders, her neck, his touch a comforting caress.

Acting on impulse, she turned to face him and his arms went around her. She stood on tiptoe and pressed her lips to his, a small whimper leaving her throat as he deepened the kiss, pulling her body to him. His mouth was warm and seeking, his tongue probing, parting her lips and delving inside. She kissed him back, meeting his tongue with hers, desperately, urgently, his firm lips searing away all the bad stuff, for just a moment, making her forget.

Reluctantly, she broke away, stepping out of Wil's embrace. "I'm sorry," she said softly, brushing a trembling hand over her still tingling lips. "This isn't what either of us needs right now."

Wil hooked a finger under her chin and lifted her face, staring intently into her eyes. "Besides getting my daughter back, being close to you, holding you, is what I need most in the world."

She gave a small shake of her head. "No. It's not a good idea. Not now."

"You're right," Wil said. "But would you stay with me tonight? I need your company, your sweetness. I promise I won't do anything, won't even touch you if you don't want me to, but will you stay with me? In my bed?"

She needed it, too. She nodded almost without being aware of it. "Yes."

****

Abby brushed her teeth, then put on a Miami Dolphin's jersey Wil gave her to sleep in. Nervously, she came out of the bathroom. Wil lay in bed with one arm bent behind his head, a dim lamp burning on the nightstand.

Normally, she knew, he slept in nothing but his boxer briefs but now he also wore a white T-shirt. She smiled, touched by the small gesture. He was doing it for her. So she wouldn't feel self-conscious. To reinforce his vow not to touch her.

While she was relieved, she had to admit, a tiny part of her was disappointed. She missed Wil's touch, his lovemaking. But, it wouldn't be right. Wouldn't feel right now that they were no longer together. It also wouldn't feel right with Lindsey missing.

Abby slid beneath the cool, thick comforter next to Wil and he flipped the light off.

"Goodnight," he said in the darkness.

"Goodnight," she responded and, for the first time in days, fell almost instantly into a dreamless sleep.

Sometime during the night, Abby woke with the weight of Wil's hand on her hip. It rested against her, burning through the cloth of the jersey...warm...tender.

She tried to lie very still, but involuntarily, she twitched with wanting. If she simply turned over on her back, his hand would...

She nearly moaned, or maybe she did, because she heard Wil's breathing change from the steady rhythm of sleep to a more shallow, labored sound.

He was awake.

Chapter Thirteen

Without speaking, Abby slowly, deliberately rotated onto her back. Almost immediately, Wil's hand slid downward. His touch was feather light, not stroking, just there, resting along her pelvic bone. She squirmed, encouraging his caress. Her breath caught in her throat as he brushed his fingers against her.

Abby turned her head to face him, their lips met, and she whimpered at the explosion of desire that shot through her. The kiss was frantic, deep, a meshing of lips and tongues.

Beneath the covers, Wil slid off his boxers, then gently rolled on top of her. She felt his erection against her thigh and sighed, lifting her hips, preparing to slip her panties off. But before she could remove them, he slid the crotch aside and entered her. She gasped at the newness of the sensation, holding onto his shoulders as he moved tenderly, slowly inside her, as if aware of the danger lurking inside her body.

Neither of them spoke. Their breathing was the only sound, and it echoed with tension and desire. It was as if the explosive resting inside her added a bizarre element of excitement, of thrill, to their coupling. She thought Wil might be thinking the same thing, but neither of them acknowledged it. If they spoke it aloud, the maniac's perversion would taint their lovemaking.

Wil stroked back and forth, increasing the pressure on her clit as he shoved the jersey up. His mouth found one hardened nipple, sucking it greedily. He moaned deep in his throat, then began to move faster. In seconds, she felt his climax explode deep inside her.

She gripped his shoulders, rubbing herself against him, seeking her own release. His hot, wet mouth tugged at her nipple, pulling gently. She gasped, then gave a small scream as her muscles tightened, then released. Wave after wave pulsed through her and she lifted her hips, pressed her body more tightly to his, feeling her orgasm throb, seeming to go on forever.

Slowly, she lowered back to the mattress as the sensation ebbed, leaving her sated, her bones like liquid fire.

"That was amazing," Abby said on a sigh, so relaxed she was barely able to form the words.

"Yeah."

"It was...different."

"Yeah," Wil said again.

He brushed the damp hair from her forehead and pulled her more tightly to him. Nestled against the warmth of his strong, solid body, she could almost believe that everything was okay. That nothing bad could touch them.

But she knew better.

Abby swallowed, squeezed her eyes tightly shut against tears, and swallowed again before she spoke. "Did it feel like the end? Of us?"

Softly, he kissed her on the ear and whispered, "Yeah."

****

Wil could still smell Abby on his skin, still feel the imprint of her shoulder blades against his chest, her soft, round bottom pressed into him...

He sighed, shifting in the seat of his truck. He'd have to find a way to stop wanting her, because he'd never have her again. By tacit agreement, they'd ended things between them for good.

He watched through the windshield as a couple of seagulls swooped in the azure sky, nearly blending in with the clouds and the white foam on the water as they dipped lower.

He was waiting for Diane to come out of Abby's office. Abby had fired her and Diane was cleaning out her belongings. Abby had told her to mail the keys when she was finished. Maybe, in spite of what she'd done, Abby trusted Diane not to take things that didn't belong to her. But it was most likely that Abby was so opposed to being around Diane, she was willing to take a chance.

Wil marveled that two people could fool him and Abby so thoroughly. Jesus, were they that imperceptive? That gullible? He shook his head. They couldn't have made worse choices if they'd shopped for friends at 'Maniacs 'R Us'.

Sighing, he peered through the windshield and watched for Diane to come out. Even though Perry's willingness to sacrifice their child had seemingly driven a wedge between the couple, Diane could possibly still lead Wil to Perry. Wil didn't know what else he could do to find Lindsey.

DNA tests were being conducted on the evidence from the mask. They would compare it to DNA taken from a search of Perry's apartment, the result of a warrant that had been issued after Diane's statement.

It would be a long while before DNA results were in, but that didn't really matter now. DNA was a moot point. Wil knew Perry had Lindsey. The only question remaining was, *where* did he have her?

Wil pulled his mind back to his quarry when she exited the building. She stopped between the swaying fronds of one of the palm trees that lined the sidewalk to re-adjust the large cardboard box she carried.

She was heading toward her car when Wil's phone rang. He answered, his body drawing up with tension when he heard the raspy, mechanical voice.

"Hey, Teddy, what's shakin'?"

Wil debated a split second before saying, "You can get rid of the voice box, Perry."

There was a slight intake of breath, then a long silence before Perry's normal voice came over the line.

"So, she broke, huh? Figured she would after you threatened to kill her child." He gave a chuckle. "I'm impressed. I mean, *I* know you wouldn't do it, but she's not so sure. She's not willing to take the chance, while I most definitely am."

"Ward Cleaver, you're not."

He chuckled again. "You make me laugh, Willie boy. That's one reason I didn't mind hanging out with you, even while I planned to destroy your life. Did Diane tell you *why* I took your daughter?"

Wil forced his voice to remain even. He didn't want to provoke Perry into hurting Lindsey. "Yes, she did, and I'm sorry. You must know I didn't do it on purpose. I had no choice. Your sister—"

"No! Don't say it. Don't you dare say it was her fault," Perry screamed.

By now, Diane had left the parking lot and Wil pulled out behind her. "Okay, okay. Just calm down. Listen, can I please talk to Lindsey? I have to know she's okay. You understand that, don't you?"

"I understand, but you can't talk to her. Not yet. I will, however, let you *hear* her."

"No!" A burst of panic shot through Wil's chest. "Please don't make her scream."

Perry chuckled. "Calm down, Willie. I wasn't gonna make her scream."

Wil heard a shuffling movement, followed by Perry's voice in the background, but he couldn't understand the words. Then, he heard Lindsey say tearfully, "I'm okay, Daddy. I love you."

Wil's heart clenched painfully and his throat tightened with unshed tears. He wanted to murder the son of a bitch, but he held onto his rage when Perry came back to the phone.

"See, Daddy, she's fine."

"Thanks for letting me hear her voice."

Perry erupted in laughter. "Oh, wow, you're being awfully civilized. Downright charitable, in fact. Pretty soon, you'll be offering me a reach-around."

"I just want to work this out without anyone getting hurt. We can do that, you know. You haven't killed anyone yet. If you release Lindsey, I can make them go easy on you. You won't do any time."

"Hmmm. You raise an interesting proposal. However, there's a flaw in your plan. You know, about me not killing anyone yet. How closely did you look into your wife's suicide?" he continued, amusement in his voice. "I know you can't see me, but I did air quotes around the word 'suicide', get it?"

Wil scowled, trying to concentrate on Diane's car and Perry's words. No, he didn't get it. What was...?

And then, suddenly, he did.

Oh, God. His body went cold and a loud buzzing started in his ears. "Did you...?" His voice was low, strained. He cleared his throat and tried again. "Did you kill my wife?"

"We have a winner! See, I've watched you for a long time, Teddy. Does that make you feel important? That I've been so interested in your life for so long?"

Wil swallowed painfully, his horrified mind digesting the information. Lindsey had said she'd heard a man that night. Wil thought it had been a dream. But it hadn't. It had been a fucking nightmare. Tara hadn't left them on purpose—she'd been taken from them by this monster.

Wil drew in a deep breath. He couldn't think about that now. He had to get Lindsey back, safe and unharmed.

And then, the bastard would pay.

"Yes, I see," Wil replied stonily.

"Now you understand how serious this is? How serious I am? Think you can play by my rules now?"

"Yes, whatever you want. I'll trade myself for Lindsey. Then you can defuse the explosives inside Abby and it will be just between you and me, like it should be."

"Sorry, wish it could be that simple, but it can't. That's not the plan I had in mind."

"Then tell me," Wil shouted, losing the hold he had on his counterfeit patience. "What the hell do I have to do to get my daughter back?"

"If you ever want to see Lindsey again," Perry replied calmly. "You have to kill the mayor."

Chapter Fourteen

Wil sat in stunned silence for a moment, not sure he'd heard correctly. Then he said, slowly, disbelievingly, "You want me to kill the mayor?"

"You got it."

"You're fucking deranged."

"Oh, I don't know about that," Perry said modestly, as if shrugging off a compliment. "But it's good to know I have your endorsement in case I get caught and plead insanity."

"Why do you want me to kill him?"

"Bingham was your captain when you killed my sister. He covered for you. Helped you get away with murder. I want him to die at the hands of his best friend. I want his family to suffer as I've suffered and I want you to live the rest of your miserable life knowing you murdered your best friend."

"I didn't murder your sister," Wil said dully. "It was self-defense. They cleared me of any wrong-doing."

"Of course they did. You pigs stick together." His voice was low, but filled with rage, and Wil worried for Lindsey.

"What, exactly, is your plan?" Wil asked.

Wanting to know, yet not wanting to.

"Now, that's much better. This is what I wanted to hear. A spirit of cooperation, enthusiasm for the task at hand." Perry went on, as if they were co-conspirators, "Here's the plan. Mayor Bingham is speaking at the statehood celebration this weekend. Sometime during his speech, you kill him. The easy part is, I don't care how you do it, or even if you get caught. It's going to be out at the beach, so your options are limitless. You can do it with a long range rife, right up close with a handgun, or from a boat. In a house, with a mouse." He chuckled at his Dr. Seuss reference. "It's televised, so I'll be watching every move. And, by the way, your girlfriend has to be there, too. The crowd will be shown, and I'd better see her there, at least catch a glimpse of her."

"Why?"

"I want her there, just in case things go wrong and I decide to end it all then. She'll be my little human grenade, all tucked in amongst the crowd. Other than that, all you have to do is make sure your friend is dead by the time the credits roll. Oh, yeah, and you can't tell the authorities, or the mayor. If I see even a hint that he knows something is amiss, Lindsey dies. And, don't think you can tell him and he'll be able to play it off like he doesn't know. That wouldn't be very smart. I don't think you want to gamble your daughter's life on his acting abilities."

"You really think I can do this? Kill my best friend?"

"You can if you want to save Lindsey."

By now, Wil had followed Diane to her house where she parked in the driveway. Wil cruised by, abandoning his surveillance. He knew he wasn't going to find Lindsey this way.

"What about Abby?" Wil asked tightly.

"Ah, Abby," Perry sighed. "That is one handsome

woman you got there, Willie boy. I mean, I've always thought she was hot, but it's funny, because I never really had any sexual urges toward her. And there's been nothing sexual about my plan, my intentions. But, when we were closed up in that steamy bathroom, and she had that tight T-shirt stretched over those pretty titties, those rosy nipples poking out at me...wow! I'm telling you, boner city."

Wil ground his teeth. The air inside the cab became oppressive and so still, so silent, it seemed Wil could hear his heart pounding in his chest. But he didn't react to Perry's words. He knew the asshole was just taunting him, trying to goad a response out of him, and Wil wouldn't give him that satisfaction.

"What about the explosives?" Wil asked.

"Oh, that. Well, the device will have to stay in her for a while. That's my guarantee of getting away. My assurance you won't come after me. As soon as I'm out of your reach, out of the reach of the law, I'll contact you and let you know how to defuse it."

"Then?"

"That's it."

"That's it? I killed your sister and you're going to let me live?"

"Let you live?" A loud burst of laughter sounded in Wil's ear. "Oh God, you're kidding, right? Let's see... I killed your wife. I traumatized your daughter—twice. I'm forcing you to kill your best friend and maybe go to prison for it. The woman you love is walking around like a fucking package from the Unabomber. All the while, I'll be living in paradise, on the coast of Australia. But, yeah, uhm, I'm letting you live." Another burst of laughter, then, in a sing-song voice, he said, "You're welcome!"

Wil didn't respond but his jaw muscles ached with the effort to control his emotions. He'd never wanted to hurt someone so much. Never wanted so badly to end a life, to slowly, painfully, make another human being cease to exist.

"Hey, Teddy, what's the matter? Not even a chuckle? Even you have to admit it's a little amusing. Nothing to say?"

"Just one thing," Wil ground out, his rage overriding his desire to placate Perry. "If you ever want to see the other side of the Pacific, you'd better kill me."

"Yeah? Well, if you don't want your one Abby to become a thousand tiny Abby's, then you'd better not threaten me again."

****

A stage had been erected on the beach with several hundred chairs sitting in the sand, facing it. Plastic red, white, and blue streamers snapped like sails in the breeze coming off the water.

Micah would arrive soon and, in the meantime, his staff made preparations.

Wil had also made preparations. He had a rifle in his pickup and a .38 in the back of his waistband.

The whole time he'd been loading ammo into the weapons, he'd kept a conversation running in his mind.

You can't be serious. Are you really planning to do this?

Of course not, I'm just going through the motions while I figure out how to fix this.

But what if you don't figure out how to fix it? What if killing Micah is the only way to save Lindsey and Abby?

He didn't respond to that one. He didn't want to say it. Didn't want to even think it. Didn't want to admit, even to himself, what his choice would be.

The scene around him was surreal. It was as if he weren't really there. That no one could see him. That he'd faded into obscurity.

People scurried back and forth between the food booths, the chairs, the portable toilets, the ocean.

Children in brightly colored swimsuits splashed in the waves that washed over the sugar white sand.

Wil spotted Abby, standing near the edge of the water, looking out over the ocean. Even from this distance, he could tell her posture was one of longing and he wondered what she was thinking. Was she wishing herself far away from Blue Harbor, from him?

"Wil?"

He whirled to find Matt Bingham standing at his elbow.

"Any news on Lindsey?" Matt asked, his eyes showing concern and a hint of wariness.

Now that Wil knew Matt had nothing to do with Lindsey's disappearance, his dislike for him seemed petty and inconsequential.

"No, nothing," Wil told him.

"I'm sorry." Matt shoved his hands in the pockets of his slacks. "I'm surprised to see you here with all you're dealing with. It's really good of you to think of my brother at a time like this."

Well, it's the least I can do. After all, I'm about to assassinate him.

Wil shrugged off the morbid thought. "I'm not staying long. I just stopped by to offer my support."

"I understand. If there's anything I can do, anything at all, let me know."

"Thank you. I'll do that." Wil's phone chirped and he jumped, the hairs on the back of his neck standing on end, the instinctive reaction telling him who was calling. He looked at Matt, stretched his frozen lips into a smile, and said, "I need to take this, see you around."

He turned his back on Matt, opened the phone, and walked away. "Yes?"

"How goes it, dude? The party's about to begin. You excited?"

"Let me talk to Lindsey." Wil felt as though

109

everything in him, his heart, his brain, his very soul was expanding and retracting, back and forth, over and over, and at any moment his body would just collapse in upon itself.

"Is everything in place?" Perry asked, ignoring Wil's request. "Have you figured out how you're gonna do it?"

The weight at the small of Wil's back seemed to warm and grow heavier, as if the gun's metal were a living, breathing thing.

"Yes." Wil's jaw tensed and he said, "But I'm not going to do a goddamned thing unless you let me talk to Lindsey."

Perry's heavy sigh came over the line. "Okay, fine. Since you asked so nicely, I guess you can talk to her, but only for a few minutes."

There was a brief silence, then, "Daddy?"

"Lindsey." The word tore from Wil's throat on a sob. His knees nearly bucked with relief at the same time an intense wave of sorrow swept through him. He wanted to say so much, but his mind was blank, he couldn't form a coherent thought. "Lindsey," he said again.

"Daddy, I'm so sorry," she sobbed, her little girls' voice ripping at his heartstrings.

"Oh, no, honey. I'm sorry. I should have protected you. I'm so very, very sorry."

"But I shouldn't have—" She stopped, took a breath. "Never mind. We don't have much time and there's something really important I want you to know. So, listen carefully, okay?"

"Sure, baby, what is it?" He seemed to have to force each word out from a throat locked tight with unshed tears. He wanted to drop to his knees in the sand and sob uncontrollably, holding her voice to him, never letting it go.

"You remember when it was raining and you told me about tears of the wounded?"

He frowned, confused. He almost said, *No, honey, remember? It was your mother who told you about that, because I wasn't around, was hardly every around, wasn't there for you, not nearly enough.*

But before he could reply, she rushed on, "Well, I didn't really understand what you meant then. But now I do. I mean, I'm there, Daddy, I'm finally there."

I'm there.

A rush of chills moved over his flesh, his blood turning to ice in his veins. She was giving him a clue.

I'm there.

"Okay, that was touching, but time's up." Perry was back on the phone and Wil jerked as if he'd been struck. The asshole's voice was an abomination, a sacrilege, after hearing the sweet music of Lindsey's. "Make it happen, dude. Her fate is in your hands." And then the line went dead.

Wil realized belatedly he hadn't told Lindsey he loved her, hadn't told her that everything would be all right.

But that was okay. It didn't matter, because now he knew where she was.

Hold on, baby girl, Daddy's coming.

Wil quickly scanned the crowd for Matt. When he spotted him, he rushed over, taking him by the arm.

Matt turned to him in surprise but before he could speak, Wil said rapidly, "Still want to help?"

Chapter Fifteen

When Abby heard the announcement over the loudspeaker that the event was about to begin, she started back up the beach. She didn't want to be here, didn't want to be around people, a threatening, evil presence among unsuspecting innocents. She was here because Perry had insisted and they had to obey. Hers and Lindsey's lives depended on it.

Perry. Diane. She still couldn't believe two people she'd trusted, that she'd known and cared about, could do something like this.

Abby noticed a figure standing further up the path she was taking, and, as if Abby's thoughts had conjured her, realized it was Diane. Abby whirled, changing directions. She'd only gone a few feet when she saw her mother standing between Abby and the seats, beaming a smile, waiting for her.

Abby felt like Indiana Jones, having to make a choice between a pit of vipers and sword-wielding assassins.

She hesitated only slightly before continuing toward her mother. As she drew closer, she marveled at how her mother never seemed to age. She'd put on some weight, the bulges showing in the grape-colored linen pantsuit she wore, but she was still a strikingly beautiful woman. Tall, with silvery blonde hair that sparkled like gold dust in the Florida sun, Charlene easily looked ten years younger than her fifty-seven.

When Abby reached her side, Charlene extended her arms and pulled Abby into a hug. Her cool, soft lips planted a kiss on Abby's cheek. "I'm so glad to see you here, darling. I was so hoping I would. How are you?"

"I'm fine, Mother, you?"

"Actually, I'm a little concerned about you." Charlene glanced toward the crowd, and tugged Abby a few feet away, out of hearing range of the other people. "Ross told me you came to the hospital."

Abby let out a frustrated breath. They'd asked him not to tell anyone what was going on, but obviously, they'd made a mistake in trusting him.

Charlene must have seen that Abby wasn't pleased, because she rushed on quickly, "He didn't tell me why, but I know you, and something must be terribly wrong or you never would have gone to Ross."

Abby shook her head, giving a small sigh of relief. "I'm fine, really. Nothing to concern yourself about."

Her mother's blue eyes peered intently at Abby. "There's something we should talk about. Something I need to tell you that I should have told you a long time ago." She frowned, and the lines in her face deepened, adding a few years to her youthful appearance. "I wanted to shield you, but that wasn't fair to me, or to Ross."

Abby frowned. "What are you talking about?"

"It's about your father."

"Look," Abby said quietly, her body tensing. "This isn't really the time or place."

"Maybe not, but it needs to be said. Ross was so happy to see you, yet at the same time, he was quite disturbed about something, although he wouldn't say what. I'm afraid you're going to take off again, and I don't want to lose you, but I'm getting too old to keep chasing you all over the country." She gave a faint smile. "Besides, I really like it here." Abby didn't return the smile and Charlene continued, "I know you haven't forgiven Ross and me for being together while I was married to your father."

"You mean while my father lay dying?" Abby asked, failing to keep the bitterness out of her voice.

Her mother's eyes filled with tears and she nodded. "Yes, but you have to understand. Stuart was a wonderful father, but he was an awful husband. He was nasty, cruel and abusive. It's true," she rushed on when Abby shook her head. "You remember that Christmas when you were ten and I was too ill to get out of bed? I wasn't able to get up with you on Christmas morning."

Abby nodded slowly. "I remember."

"I didn't get out of bed because your father had kicked me so hard in the kidneys I couldn't stand. I didn't find out until later that day, when I finally went to the hospital, that I was bleeding internally."

Tears stung Abby's eyes and nausea rose in her throat. "He didn't...he wouldn't..." She shook her head, not able to finish.

"I'm sorry, honey, but he did. It's the truth. That was the day I met Ross. He wanted to report it to the police, but I wouldn't let him. I didn't want your world destroyed." She sighed and swiped at the tears on her cheeks. "Ross and I fell in love. Ross showed me what it felt like to be *truly* loved. He treated me like something to be treasured, unlike your father, who treated me like a punching bag, like something to be ground under his boot heel. I was trying to gather the courage to divorce him when he became ill. I couldn't leave him, but I couldn't give up Ross, either. I know it was wrong, but I wanted you to see that it wasn't as wrong as it might have seemed."

Abby didn't respond. She stared at her mother in silence. As awful as it was, as unbelievably horrific, Abby did believe. She saw the truth in her mother's eyes and she felt sick.

She heard a crackle of static, followed by a voice over the speaker announcing that the ceremony was beginning.

"Thanks for telling me," Abby finally managed.

Turning away from her mother, Abby made her way to where the crowd was settling in for the ceremony. She had to make herself visible so Perry would know she was there.

As Abby took her seat, it occurred to her that she should have told her mother she forgave her and Ross, and that she loved her.

She should have told her mother she understood. That when you find the kind of love she had with Ross, you should do whatever it takes to hold onto it.

Even if it meant risking your life.

****

Wil listened to the speech on the radio as he sped toward the beach house, sixty miles from Blue Harbor. He should be there in less than half an hour.

Matt was introducing his brother and was currently relating a story from when he had been six and Micah eight. Micah had poured water on the mattress beneath a sleeping Matt, making their parents think Matt had wet the bed.

This was the fourth such anecdote Matt had shared. Even over the radio, Wil could detect the sounds of restless shuffling and throat clearing. Wil gave a wry grin. At the rate Matt was going, Wil could be all the way to Texas by the time his stories reached their teen years.

Wanting to ensure the speech was delayed, Wil had enlisted Matt's help. If Micah finished, alive and well, before Wil reached Lindsey, Perry would kill her.

Wil was making record time, pushing the speed limit extra hard. He hoped like hell he'd gotten Lindsey's message right. Otherwise, Lindsey—and Abby—would still die.

When Wil and his family had lived in the rat race that was Miami, Tara had pleaded with him to buy a house on the ocean so they could live in a safe, peaceful area. He'd kept promising her he would, but never had.

As often as she could, Tara would take Lindsey and escape to the beach house. It had ended up being the place where she died. Afterward, Wil had decided to honor Tara's wish, too little, too late—as usual. But he couldn't live in the house where she'd died, so he'd sold the beach house and bought the one in Blue Harbor.

Had Perry been the one to buy it? Wil had sold it through a realtor and had never met the buyer. It was definitely a possibility. Either that, or Perry had simply broken in.

Or, he wasn't at the beach house at all, and Wil was fucked.

When Wil was less than a mile from the house, he heard a female voice on the radio diplomatically cut Matt off, thank him, then introduce the mayor. It didn't matter now. Wil would be there in a couple of minutes.

He parked a few streets away and made the rest of his way on foot. He approached from the southwest corner, remembering from his brief visits that there were no windows on that side.

The house's white paint was peeling and weeds sprouted in the too-tall grass. Tara's garden she'd so lovingly tended was now a patch of dirt and dead plants.

Wil looked out over the water, not seeing any swimmers or boaters in the area. The nearest neighbor was almost a mile down the beach.

They were alone, he and the occupants of the beach house.

Hopefully, Perry and Lindsey.

With gun drawn, and his back to the outside wall, Wil slid around to the front of the house and halted.

Perry's beloved Firebird was in the driveway.

Chapter Sixteen

Wil stood next to the large picture window, staying flush against the house. If Perry were inside, even if he looked out the window, he wouldn't see Wil.

Standing motionless, Wil listened. He heard a male voice but the words were muffled. He thought the sound might be coming from a television. Perhaps the mayor's speech.

Lifting his head, Wil glimpsed curtains drawn over the windows. He couldn't look inside, couldn't pinpoint Lindsey's location. Couldn't run in with gun blazing.

He'd have to make Perry come outside.

Wil crouched and stayed along the outside edge of the house. He skirted the far side of the driveway and crept to the car, where he removed his jacket and wrapped it around his hand. He scanned the area, ensuring there were no onlookers who might be caught in the crossfire, then rammed his fist through the passenger window, shattering glass that rained like diamonds on his head. A strident, uneven wail pierced the silence, sounding so loud, Wil had to cover his ears against the assault.

The door to the beach house flew open and Perry half stumbled, half ran out, wildly waving a pistol, bellowing, "What the fuck. Who's there? What the fuck did you do to my car?"

Perry pressed the button on a key fob, silencing the alarm. The sudden stillness was almost as deafening as the incessant noise had been.

Perry sprinted to the Firebird and placed both palms on the hood, his expression one of confusion and grief. Before he could notice the broken window and make his way to the other side of the Firebird, Wil dropped into a prone position on the ground, aimed underneath the car, and fired two quick rounds into Perry's ankle.

Perry made a sound somewhere between a groan and a shriek, falling to the ground. Wil rounded the car and jumped on the downed man, slamming his fist into Perry's face so hard, his head slammed against the pavement.

Perry yelped and thrashed beneath Wil, blood mingling with the snot and tears that poured from his nose and eyes. Perry fiercely scrubbed his hands over his face, struggling to get away, attempting to see his attacker.

When his vision cleared, he recognized Wil and his terror and bewilderment morphed into fury. "You motherfucker!" he raged. "What the fuck did you do? How did you find me?"

Wil climbed off him and jerked him to his feet by the collar of his grass-stained polo shirt. When Perry's injured foot touched the ground, his leg buckled, but Wil pulled him upright.

"Move," Wil growled into Perry's ear. He shoved him toward the house. Perry stumbled through the door and Wil followed.

Wil scanned the room. The decor was different than he remembered. Tara had filled the beach house with white wicker furniture and paisley print cushions. There'd been lots of tropical plants, and brightly colored throw rugs had adorned the shiny, hardwood floor.

Now the floors were bare, the wood faded and peeling. A blue sofa rested against one wall, facing a twenty-inch TV on a black chrome stand. Adjacent to the sofa was a wooden kitchen chair with a slatted back.

In the chair sat Lindsey. Her hands were behind her, a gag duct-taped over her mouth. When she saw Wil, her eyes became enormous liquid pools. A look of such joy and relief filled them that Wil felt tears surface in his own.

His happiness at seeing Lindsey alive was momentarily replaced by a white hot fury more intense than anything he'd felt before.

He tightened his hold on Perry's collar, choking him for a moment before slamming the butt of the .38 into the back of his head. Perry went down like a discarded bag of garbage.

Wil rushed over to Lindsey and peeled away the tape as gently as he could, but she still winced as it pulled at her delicate skin. When her mouth was uncovered, she said, "Daddy! I knew you'd come. You got my hint, didn't you?"

Wil spoke as he worked at the ropes binding her to the chair. "Yes, baby, I did. That was very clever of you. I'm so proud."

When Lindsey was free, she tore from the chair and threw herself against him. Wil's arms closed around her and he squeezed her tightly, holding her while she sobbed into his chest.

"I'm so sorry," he murmured. "God, I'm so sorry. I love you, baby. I'm so glad you're okay." He placed a kiss on the top of her soft hair, smelling the faint scent of shampoo and sweat.

"It's okay, Daddy. Everything's okay now."

He reluctantly separated from her and took her

shoulders, looking her in the eye. "Listen, I want you to go, run. My truck is parked out on Ballinger Road. Get to it and lock yourself inside until me or the police come, you understand?"

But Lindsey was already shaking her head. "I'm not leaving you. Come with me. Please, come with me."

Perry moaned and Wil turned. Perry was on all fours, trying to rise to his feet. Wil turned back to Lindsey and gave her a little shake. "Run, honey, run now. I'll be fine."

Wil placed a quick kiss on her forehead and went back to Perry. His eyes were batting open and their glazed reddish orbs shot fire at Wil.

Wil jerked him to his feet and slammed him against the wall. He shoved the gun into Perry's ribs. "Where's the detonator?"

"Fuck you."

"You shithead little cocksucker," Wil bit out softly, aware that Lindsey hadn't yet obeyed his command. She was still in the room. "Tell me where it is, or the next few minutes are going to be very painful for you."

"Go to hell," Perry screamed, unconcerned about Lindsey's delicate sensibilities. "I don't give a fuck what you do to me. The bitch is still gonna die. You're gonna pay for murdering my sister."

Wil gripped Perry's throat and squeezed, still jamming the gun into his side. "Wanna know something? You're right. I killed your sister. And here's the beauty part of it. This will give you something to think about when your fellow inmates are shoving a broom handle so far up your ass you get splinters in your throat. I know about the money you got from your parents' deaths. I know they got the money from the life insurance policy on your dead sister. We searched your apartment and I found it. And, guess what? It's mine now." That was a lie. The cash had been found, but it was locked up in evidence. Wil hadn't touched it. "So, you might say, not only did I kill your sister. I'm actually getting *paid* for it."

Perry let out an enraged scream, bucking and jerking at Wil's hold. Tears poured from his eyes and a string of expletives flew from his lips.

Still aware of his daughter behind him, Wil said, "Lindsey, dammit, run. Run now!"

"Abby's gonna die, no matter what." Perry choked out the words around the grip Wil had on his throat. A satisfied gleam came into his eyes. "Right after I hung up the phone, I set the timer on the explosive. I knew it would give me time to get away, and you'd still pay, maybe die, maybe not. The blast will kill Abby and whoever is around her."

Wil stared at him for a moment in disbelief. "You didn't...she's not..." He loosened his hold, shock and helplessness momentarily making him numb.

Wil was aware of the sound of a door opening and turned briefly to see Lindsey disappear out the back. Perry took advantage of his distraction and shoved against him.

Wil almost lost his hold on the gun, but tightened his hand around the butt as he stumbled back. Perry rushed Wil and knocked him to the ground, landing on top and punching him in the jaw.

Wil's head jerked and pain exploded in his cheek, but it was just enough to snap him out of the inertia that gripped him. He slammed his fist into Perry's already bloody face and knocked him backward. Wil lunged on top of him and shoved the gun in his neck.

"Tell me how the fuck to stop it."

Perry shook his head. "You have two hours, asshole. Figure it out for yourself."

Wil heard movement behind him and looked around. Lindsey was slowly entering through the door from which she'd escaped.

Diane stood behind her, holding a pistol.

Chapter Seventeen

"Let him go, Wil," Diane commanded.

Shit! Wil looked at his daughter. Her face was bone-white and she trembled violently. One knuckle of a crooked index finger was clamped tightly between her teeth.

Wil climbed off Perry and stood, the gun hanging limply in his right hand. He tried to give Lindsey a reassuring smile but it probably looked more like a petrified grimace.

Perry rose, wiping the blood from his face. "Oh, baby," He gasped out a relieved sigh. "God, am I glad to see you."

He stepped toward her but Diane lifted the gun, pointing it at his chest.

"Don't move!" she screamed, her voice sharp with venom. "You sorry son of a bitch. You were going to let my child, *our* child, die."

"No, sweetie, no way. I knew Wil wouldn't hurt her. I wouldn't—"

Diane placed her other hand on the grip of the pistol. "Shut up."

Wil eased away from Perry and calmly said to Diane, "Okay. We have him now. He's going to prison. Let's call the police."

"What about Abby?" Diane asked, her gaze still on Perry. "Because of him, she's going to die."

"We'll figure something out. We'll make him tell—"

"I'm not telling you jack shit," Perry spat. He said to Diane, "They have to pay. You know that, don't you? He murdered my sister!"

Diane's mouth stretched into a humorless smile. "Ah yes, your beloved sister. Good news, Perry. I've arranged a reunion."

Before Wil could react, the gun went off. A neat, round hole appeared in Perry's forehead and his eyes widened, then he dropped to the ground.

Wil looked from Perry's still twitching corpse to Diane, stunned surprise keeping him momentarily frozen.

Diane's gun hand still pointed at Perry and tears rolled down her ashen cheeks, but there was no emotion in her voice when she said to Wil, "I'll wait for the police. Go save Abby."

****

Wil used his cell phone to call Abby as he and Lindsey raced to the truck. "Abby, hon, listen to me carefully," he said when she answered. "I need to tell you something very important."

"Yes?" Her voice held puzzlement and a hint of concern.

"Do you feel any different?"

"Different? No. Why?"

He didn't want to tell her about the bomb being detonated, didn't want her to panic, but he had to tell her something. "Where are you?"

"I'm at home. Wil, what's going on?"

"I'll explain everything when I get there. Right now, just sit tight. Be very careful, just stay put and take it easy."

"Oh, God."

"It's okay, hon. It's going to be okay."

"It's been detonated, hasn't it?"

"Everything's going to be fine. Don't panic. I'll be there soon and we'll get that thing out of you."

"Oh, God," she said again, her voice a choked whisper. "How long before it goes off?"

"Abby, stay with me, baby. That doesn't matter because I'll be there shortly with help. We're going to take care of everything. You have to trust me."

Her next words scared him more than anything else had.

"Wil, I love you," she whispered.

Then the line went dead.

Chapter Eighteen

Wil fished out the business card Ross Novak had given him and dialed, keeping an eye on the road, and on Lindsey, who sat silent and pale in the passenger seat.

He identified himself when Ross answered, then asked, "Where are you?"

"I'm at home."

"Give me your address. I'm coming by. What do you have there in the way of surgical equipment, anesthesia, that sort of thing?"

"Here? Nothing."

"Okay. We'll have to go by the hospital. I'll need you to call them and have someone gather what you'll need. Is your wife there?"

"Yes, she is. Need for what? What's this about?"

"It's Abby. The bomb's been detonated and we have..." He looked at the clock on the dashboard. "...an hour and forty-five minutes to get it out of her and defuse it. If you can get it out, I can defuse it. Can my daughter stay with your wife?"

"Your daughter? She's okay? She's safe?"

"Yes. And if you'll help me, we'll save yours."

Novak was quiet for a moment, but Wil could

hear his breathing and it sounded like he was struggling with tears. His voice was raw when he spoke. "Of course I'll help you. Of course your daughter can stay here. I'll call the hospital now."

Novak gave Wil the address and Wil disconnected the call.

Wil tried Abby's phone again, aware that making calls while driving wasn't the wisest thing to do, but the urgency of the situation took precedence over road safety.

The call went straight to voicemail. She had her phone off.

Don't panic, it's okay. Maybe she's there waiting like you told her to be, but she's on another line. Maybe the phone was dead. Maybe...

He tried to convince himself of a number of non-frightening scenarios, but he knew better.

Wil, I love you, she'd said.

Not long ago, that had been exactly what he'd wanted to hear her say. But things were different now. He'd come to realize she was right to end things. All he could offer her was uncertainty and danger. After what she'd been through, she deserved peace...security. No matter how he'd tried to run from it, he was a cop. One day, he'd return to that life. He knew Abby couldn't handle it and it wasn't fair for him to ask her to.

Mainly, he hadn't wanted to hear those words from her because she'd never said them before, and it scared him that she now felt the need. She'd sounded resigned...fatalistic. He pushed that thought aside. She was okay, she had to be. He'd help her, then he'd say goodbye, set her free.

When they arrived at Novak's house, Ross met them outside. An older, attractive version of Abby followed behind.

Quick introductions were made, then Wil hugged his daughter. Lindsey clung to him until he finally had to pry her arms away. He held her face in his hands. "I'll be back, sweetheart. You'll be fine here with Charlene, okay?"

She nodded and he left her there, praying he wasn't abandoning her too soon after her ordeal, knowing he didn't have a choice.

He and Ross sped to the hospital. Wil waited impatiently in the pickup while Ross disappeared inside.

It wasn't long, just under ten minutes by the dashboard clock, but it seemed like hours before Ross reappeared, holding a white plastic bag with large green letters printed on the side that read, 'St. John's Hospital'. Minutes later, they pulled up to Abby's house.

Her car wasn't in the driveway and Wil's heart plummeted to his shoes.

He banged on her door, rationalizing why her car wasn't there, but she still could be. She didn't respond and he tried the knob. It was unlocked.

Inside, instead of Abby, he found a letter.

> *Dear Wil,*
>
> *I'm doing what has to be done.*
>
> *Please don't try to find me and don't blame yourself. I know you. You would try to save me and I can't let you. Lindsey needs you. She's already lost one parent. She shouldn't lose another.*
>
> *It's not fair to you, either, to lose two women you love in one lifetime. You deserve better. And, yes, I know you love me, even though I wouldn't let you say it. I love you, too.*
>
> *Tell my stepfather and my mother I love them, and I'm so sorry I only recently realized how much.*
>
> *Goodbye,*
> *Abby*

Wil felt a slow steady hum start in his head, blocking out all other sounds.

He looked around the room and the desperately ridiculous hope surfaced that maybe she was just hiding from him, not realizing how limited their time was.

Novak took the letter from Wil's shaking hand.

"Oh God," he moaned when he read it. "Where could she be?"

Wil rushed to the door. "She's on the water. She has to be. It's the only place she'd feel she wouldn't harm anyone else."

But when he ran to the dock, her boat was in its slip. His shoulders slumped in defeat. What now? They were running out of time and he was at a dead end.

His choice of phrase made a chill run over his spine.

No. She wouldn't die. He wouldn't let her.

"Little Match Girl," Novak said and Wil turned to him, narrowing his eyes in confusion.

"I beg your pardon?" Wil said.

"The boat. I gave it to her a few years ago for her birthday, but she didn't want to take it. It's actually a yacht. I named her Little Match Girl because that was Abby's favorite story when she was a child. I bet she's on it."

Wil decided not to think too deeply about that. From what he remembered from story time with Lindsey, The Little Match Girl hadn't ended all that happily. "Where did she moor it?"

"I don't know," Novak said frantically. "Maybe somewhere nearby?"

Wil flipped open his cell phone and called a friend at the Coast Guard. "Jim, need a favor. Would you issue a possible distress signal on a forty-foot Sea Ray?" He relayed the information as Novak gave it to him. "Registered as Little Match Girl out of

Florida. No, don't have the registration number, sorry."

As he spoke, Wil hurried inside and found the keys to the Bayliner in their usual spot by the door. He grabbed them and rushed back out, hanging up his cell after Jim assured him they'd report back if they found the boat.

"How long will it take for her to go under with the anesthesia?" he asked Ross as they climbed aboard the Bayliner.

"It will take effect immediately."

"And to perform the surgery?"

Novak shrugged. "Hard to say for sure. I won't know until I get inside, but anywhere from thirty minutes to an hour would be my guess."

Wil looked at his watch as he guided the boat onto the water. Half an hour or more for the surgery, at least five minutes to defuse the bomb, depending on what type of explosive it was.

That left them, at the most, forty-five minutes to find Abby and convince her to let them save her life.

A cold sweat broke out on Wil's skin in spite of the ocean throwing a mist of cool water onto the boat. His bowels clenched with fear as he clutched the cell phone, willing it to ring with news the coast guard had found Abby.

When the call came, he nearly melted with relief.

They had less than an hour.

Chapter Nineteen

The Little Match Girl was a beautiful boat and Wil had the irrationally mundane thought that Abby was a fool for refusing such a magnificent gift.

He pulled the Bayliner up beside it and shouted for Abby.

Silence.

A rush of panic swept through him. Abby may have decided not to wait for the explosion. She may have ended her life already, loathe to tick off the seconds until she died a violent and horrific death.

His heart nearly stopped when he saw her appear above them. Her face was pinched, and even from this distance, he could see her beautiful brown eyes were dull with grief. She wore jeans and a loose fitting yellow blouse. She looked so lost, so vulnerable.

"You need to leave," she said quietly, so quietly Wil barely heard her above the sounds of the waves and the creaking of the boat.

"Abby, we're here to help you but we don't have much time," Wil said calmly. "You need to cooperate and let us save you."

"Is Lindsey...?"

"Lindsey's safe. She's with your mother."

Abby's eyes closed. "Thank God." She opened them again and said, "I appreciate what you're both trying to do. But I can't let you risk your lives for me. Mom and Lindsey need you. I'm ready for whatever happens. Please don't worry about me."

Tears moved from Wil's throat to his eyes, threatening to spill over. He couldn't speak.

"Abby, sweetie," Novak said. "You mean the world to both of us, and to your mother. There's no way we're leaving you to die." His breath hitched and Wil knew he was close to tears, too. "Dammit, we're running out of time."

"Then, just go," Abby said, a sob tearing through the words. "Please, just go."

"No. We're not leaving," Wil said harshly. "We'll circle the ship until we all die if that's the way you want it. The longer you argue, the more you risk all our lives."

Abby's features tensed, then crumpled. Wil watched in grateful relief as she hurried over and lowered the steps, moving back so they could come aboard.

When Wil climbed on deck, he pulled her into his arms and brushed a hand down her silky hair. With his lips against her ear, he whispered, "I won't let anything happen to you, I promise."

Novak hurried toward the galley. "Follow me. We need to get started right away."

They walked down a steep, short flight of stairs into the cabin. A bed hung from one end of the wall and Novak motioned for Abby to lie down. She did and he opened his bag.

"How much time do we have?" she asked shakily.

Wil looked at his watch. He didn't want to answer.

"How much?" she demanded.

133

Sighing, he responded, "We have just under an hour before the explosives are due to detonate. It will take thirty minutes, maybe more, for your stepfather to remove the device. At least five for me to defuse."

Tears swam in her eyes but she nodded slowly and said to Ross, "Don't wait for me to go completely under. I can handle the pain. Just get it done."

As she spoke, her stepfather injected a needle in her vein and depressed the plunger. "You'll be fine, Abby girl, I promise."

Her eyelids fluttered and her words slurred. "We'll all be fine," she whispered, and went to sleep.

****

Slowly Abby opened her eyes, for a moment, befuddled. Then memory returned. She sensed someone next to her. She turned her head to find Wil sitting beside her bed, his hand wrapped warmly around hers.

"Did I make it?" she asked, her mouth dry, her words barely audible.

"What do you think?" Wil smiled gently.

"Well, I hurt like hell, and you're certainly no angel, so it can't be heaven. I'm either alive, or you and I were *both* very naughty people."

Wil laughed. "You're alive, thank God."

"The explosive?"

"It was like an episode of 'Alias'. I defused it with mere seconds to spare."

"Sorry I missed that," Abby slurred, her eyes drifting shut. When she wasn't so tired, she would tell Wil she'd been wrong. She wouldn't be so foolish to throw away what they had when she'd been lucky enough to find love again. "What happened to Perry?"

Wil blew a breath out between clenched teeth and said, "Diane shot him. They have her in custody now. She told Ray she followed me from the celebration, thinking I might be heading to where Perry was. She didn't get there right away because she lost my trail. I set the alarm off on Perry's car to draw him outside and Diane heard it. She found us and..." he trailed off, shrugging as if to say, 'you know the rest'.

Abby nodded slowly. She was hurt by Diane's betrayal, but glad it was all over. So glad everyone was safe.

"Someone wants to see you," Wil whispered, still holding her hand. "You feel up to it?"

She nodded and opened her eyes. She was still sluggish, but the joy of being alive and out of danger made her feel she could conquer the world.

Abby smiled when Lindsey came into the cabin and stood beside Wil. "I'm glad you're okay," Lindsey said.

"I'm glad you're okay, too," Abby replied.

Lindsey suddenly began to cry and she dropped to her knees beside Abby's bed. "I'm sorry I was so awful to you."

"It's okay, honey."

"No, it's not." Lindsey shook her head vehemently. "I've grown up a lot in the past few days. The whole time that asshole had me, I was thinking, 'man, and I thought I had it bad before.' I thought about all the terrible things in the world and how those things are *real* problems. Not the fact that my dad has a girlfriend. And you...you're awesome. Deep down, I always thought that but I wouldn't let myself really like you." She gave a watery smile. "I've learned there are worse things than your dad having a girlfriend. I was stupid and I'm sorry."

"Apology accepted. Thank you."

Lindsey nodded and brushed her hands across her cheeks, wiping away tears. "Okay, then. I'll let you guys talk." She gave her father a tight hug.

135

"Love you, Daddy."

"Love you, too, baby girl. I'll be up in a minute."

After Lindsey left, an awkward silence settled over them. Abby was the first to break it. "She's a good kid."

"Yeah."

Silence again.

"Wil, I was wrong. About us. I want to try again. I don't want to lose you."

Wil sighed and dropped his gaze to the floor, gently disentangling his hand from hers.

Panic beat at her heart and she knew then, it was too late. Wil had changed his mind. He didn't want her anymore. "Wil? What is it?"

He shook his head, not looking at her. "You were right, Abby. We shouldn't be together. It almost got you killed."

"But..." she didn't know what to say. Didn't know how to fight for him. She said, "Are you punishing me for ending things with you? If you are, I understand, and I'll wait. But please, don't punish me forever."

"Punishing you?" Wil lifted his head, his expression agonized. "I'm punishing *me*. I can't do this, Abby, can't do 'us'. I can't cause you any more pain, any more danger. It's best this way. When Lindsey turns eighteen, I'm going back to the force. You should live in peace."

"You're wrong. I tried to avoid violence and look what happened. It found me anyway. I don't want to hide anymore."

"It found you because of me."

She stared at him through the tears swimming in her eyes. She was searching for words to make him change his mind when a clatter at the door caught her attention. Two EMT's entered the cabin.

"They're taking you to a hospital," Wil said. "They want to check you over and keep you for a few days just to make sure everything's okay."

Abby nodded but didn't speak.

Wil moved aside to make room for the EMT's.

"Goodbye, Abby," he said quietly.

This time, she knew he meant it.

Chapter Twenty

The hospital released Abby two days after the surgery. She hadn't heard from Wil, didn't expect to. She knew it was time to heal her broken heart along with her body.

Abby was delighted when Lindsey accompanied Charlene to pick her from the hospital. Apparently, the two of them had formed some kind of bond during all of this. Abby wondered if it would cause any type of awkwardness since she and Wil were no longer together.

"Hey, Abby, how are you feeling?" Lindsey asked, and she looked so much like her father, it made Abby ache.

"I'm good, thanks."

"You sure seem quiet," Charlene commented.

"It's a hospital, Mom. We're supposed to be quiet."

Charlene harrumphed, looking shrewdly at Abby, but didn't say anything.

The nurse wheeled Abby outside and Lindsey helped her into the back seat of Charlene's Lincoln Continental.

The ride was oddly silent and Abby wasn't

inclined to change that. She stared out the window, watching the people outside their homes, or walking along the town sidewalk, seemingly happy, content. None of them appeared to be living with a hollow ache that Abby knew must show on the outside, as great as the pain was on the inside. Pain that didn't have anything to do with surgery.

She only roused when her mother passed the turnoff to her road. "Mom, you missed the turn."

"What's that, dear?" her mother asked, although Abby knew she must have heard her in the dead silence of the car.

"You missed my turnoff," Abby repeated, irritation now entering her voice. She just wanted to get home. Wanted to be alone, for the first time in days, to wallow in her misery.

"That's nice," her mother replied.

Good Lord, what was her problem?

They slowed and turned onto Huntington Way. Abby looked sharply at her mother, then at Lindsey, but they both pointedly ignored her.

Abby tensed. This was the way to Wil's house.

"What's going on?" Abby asked. When her mother didn't answer, she said, "Lindsey? What's going on?"

By then, they were turning onto Wil's road. His driveway was just a few houses up and, sure enough, the Lincoln slowed and pulled into it.

"What the *hell* is going on?" Abby demanded. "I'm tired. I need to be at home and if this is your idea of a joke, it's not very funny." She wasn't sure to whom she spoke, but thought they both deserved her wrath.

Her mother rested one arm on the back of the front seat and twisted so she could meet Abby's gaze. "You're going to talk to him."

"What? Why? We've already talked. It's over. We both decided that was best."

139

Lindsey shook her head, making her ponytail swing against her cheeks. "It's *not* best. I haven't seen Dad cry since Mom died. But twice since they took you to the hospital, I've caught him with tears in his eyes. He's miserable without you and he won't make the move, so you have to."

"Lindsey, hon," Abby said gently, patiently. "This isn't some little tiff we need to get past. There are things involved that you can't possibly understand. Reasons why we can't be together. We all just have to accept it."

"Bullshit," Charlene said and Abby's head whipped toward her. She'd never heard her mother swear. "That's the biggest line of crap I've ever heard. You two love each other, bottom line. Go talk to him and quit acting like a wuss."

"Mom, maybe now isn't a good time. I'm tired. I was just released from the hospital."

"Walking will help you regain your strength. Get out."

Abby sighed and jerked the car door open. She wouldn't argue. She'd talk to Wil, go back and tell the busybodies it hadn't done any good, and go home to lick her wounds.

Climbing out of the car, Abby slammed the door behind her, just to show them she wasn't happy about their little plan.

She looked up at the house and her breath caught in her throat.

She was going to see Wil again.

Although she'd longed to see him, she was terrified at the prospect.

She started toward the steps, but heard noise coming from the back of the house and went around. Wil stood there, shirtless, his back to her, sanding a surfboard. The muscles in his shoulders jumped with his movements and the wind ruffled his hair. For a moment, she just stood there, watching him, letting the sight of him act as balm to her senses.

He must have felt her presence, because he turned. When his gaze met hers, the hazel depths of his eyes gleamed for a moment with something like joy before they shuttered over, hiding whatever emotion had surfaced.

"Abby? Is everything okay?"

No. I love you and you don't want to be with me and my heart is breaking.

"Yes," she said around the knot in her throat.

"What are you doing here?"

She shrugged and gestured toward the front of the house. "My mother and Lindsey picked me up from the hospital. They thought we should talk."

He turned away from her and continued sanding. "Lindsey can't seem to get it through her head that you and I are no longer together."

"I know," Abby said. "Quite a change from a week ago."

"Yeah. Kids. Never satisfied."

"She's right."

"What?" Wil asked, still keeping his back to her.

"We should be together. I love you."

She saw his shoulders stiffen and the sanding stopped. He slowly turned to face her. "Abby, I told you, when Lindsey turns eighteen, I'm going back to being a cop."

She forced a lightness to her voice. "That's four years from now. Who knows what'll happen between now and then?" She grinned as she threw his earlier words back at him. "You didn't think I was going to marry you, did you?"

He smiled and the smile did the same funny things to her insides it always had. "You're not?"

She shook her head. "I just want to try again. Take it slowly and see if our love is as strong as I think it is."

He sighed and his eyes held a pained look before

he glanced away, shaking his head. "No matter how much I love you, it won't work."

"You're that sure?" she demanded. "So sure you won't even give it a try?"

"You couldn't handle me being a cop."

She gave a strangled laugh, tears close to the surface. "I carried a bomb around in my womb for a week. I went out on a boat alone to explode into a million pieces. I think dating a cop is pretty mild compared to that."

He was silent for a moment, then his gaze swung to her and she saw something different in his expression. Something hopeful. "What about marrying one?"

Her breath caught in her throat. "Marrying?"

"Lindsey thinks that's what we need to do."

She smiled. "Do you do everything your daughter says?"

"Sometimes, she's smarter than her old man. But I'm not doing it because she told me to."

"Then why?"

He shrugged and said, "Because I miss you. Because my life is empty without you and I'm tired of punishing myself. Tired of hurting over you."

"Yeah?"

"Yeah."

The tears flowed freely now and Abby didn't even try to wipe them away.

Wil dropped the sander and pulled her to him, staring down at her. "Abby..."

He didn't say more. He didn't have to, because he kissed her and in his kiss, she felt the same happiness, the same yearning that churned within her.

His arms tightened, holding her against his heart and at that moment, all was right with the world.

Abby had come home.